OUTLAW BARBECUE

Slocum found that his horse wanted to go down into the ravine, proof that the outlaws and their camp were near.

He dragged out his six-gun and listened hard in case any of the rustlers had heard him.

When the scent of burning mesquite reached him, Slocum tugged at the horse's reins, drawing it to one side. He tethered the horse securely and advanced on foot.

Slocum immediately found himself in the center of a dozen men. Their campfire had died out, leaving behind the lingering odor of mesquite he had smelled only minutes before.

Slocum had thought their camp would be farther off. He was wrong.

Slocum found a dozen rifles and six-shooters pointing at him. He had nowhere to run.

JAKE LOGAN

THE LADY GAMBLER

J

JOVE BOOKS, NEW YORK

THE LADY GAMBLER

A Jove Book / published by arrangement with
the author

PRINTING HISTORY
Jove edition / March 1996

The Putnam Berkley World Wide Web site address is
http://www.berkley.com

ISBN: 0-515-11827-3

A JOVE BOOK®
Jove Books are published by The Berkley Publishing Group,
200 Madison Avenue, New York, New York 10016.
JOVE and the "J" design are trademarks
belonging to Jove Publications, Inc.

PRINTED IN THE UNITED STATES OF AMERICA

10 9 8 7 6 5 4 3 2 1

THE LADY
GAMBLER

1

"Death, death everywhere around us," Doc Bond grumbled. "Look out there. See it?"

John Slocum shrugged. He needed the job riding shotgun messenger for the Abilene Stagecoach Company. What he didn't need was the driver's constant rambling. The dust was bad, the intense heat burned Slocum's face to leather, the wind sliced at his eyes, but the worst of the lot were Doc Bond's tall tales about raiding Comanches and the road agents and all the rest. And if, one more time, Slocum heard the story of how the driver had earned the nickname "Doc" by tending half the town of Fort Griffin when it came down with cholera, he might just chuck the driver out into the burning hell he was so fond of describing.

"Mark my words, Slocum," the grizzled driver said, taking time to turn his head and spit. Some of the tobacco juice caught on the wind and splattered against the side of the coach, spraying the three passengers inside with brown sludge. Slocum didn't hear any complaints, though. Neither of the men nor the attractive young lady inside might have noticed the tobacco rain since they'd dropped the canvas flaps over the open windows to keep out some of the choking Texas dust.

"Scorpions," Doc Bond rattled on, oblivious to Slocum turning away to study the slow passage of sand and rocky hills. "And rattlers, both slitherin' round on their bellies and the kind what walk upright, if you catch my drift."

"Road agents," Slocum acknowledged, bored.

"Right you are. It's a true pleasure having a shotgun messenger ridin' along who appreciates the dangers out here. Tarantulas. And summer heat that'll bleach your bones 'fore you know it. Yes, sir, I been drivin' the Abilene–Fort Griffin road for well nigh a year now, and no two runs are the same."

"Each is different," Slocum said, wishing the trip was over. Fort Griffin was hardly the shining metropolis of the West but it was a damned sight better than sitting next to this garrulous old coot. Besides, Slocum could use a drop or two of whiskey to wet his whistle. Their desert bag sloshing against the side of the stagecoach was almost empty, the passengers having taken more than their fair share of the precious water inside. "Each is dangerous."

Doc Bond turned toward Slocum and cocked his head to one side, squinting at his companion through his good eye. "You ain't sassin' me, now, are you, boy?"

"I'd never do a thing like that," Slocum said, fighting to keep sarcasm from his voice. He shifted his feet on the express box. As heavy as that strongbox felt when he'd hefted it back in Abilene, it had to have a thousand dollars worth of gold in it. Slocum didn't know for sure, but he reckoned it contained a payroll for the fort. Mostly, they carried nothing more exciting than a large canvas bag or two stuffed with letters. The U.S. Mail was an important customer for the Abilene Stagecoach Company, but the notion of protecting a few scraps of paper seemed ridiculous to Slocum.

The idea of dying for what rode under his boots was even more absurd. He had done his share of robbing in his day, but Slocum had put that behind him. Guarding the box was his job, but he wasn't as committed to it as Doc Bond sounded about his job as driver. And Slocum sure as hell wasn't going to give his life, if it came to that. The soldiers at Fort Griffin might be pissed off at missing a payday, but they'd get over it. Slocum knew Doc Bond was right about one thing. Death was final.

"No, sir, a man wouldn't last a day out there among the prickly pear cactus without water. This here prairie looks peaceable enough, but it is vicious," Doc Bond went on, as if Slocum were a greenhorn and had no idea how to survive in the arid grasslands.

Slocum shifted, put the shotgun he carried into the box beside him, then stared ahead at the winding brown ribbon of dusty road. He pulled up his red bandanna to protect his nose and mouth and tugged at the brim of his new silver belly Stetson to keep the dust from his eyes.

He rode along like this, ignoring the driver's continual rambling, trying to keep the grit from his mouth, and rocking slowly with the motion of the stagecoach.

What it was that brought Slocum fully erect and grabbing for the shotgun, he didn't know. Slocum had always trusted his sixth sense when it warned of danger, and now it was screaming.

"What's wrong, boy?" demanded Doc Bond. The driver reined back a tad, giving the horses a rest as they struggled up a low hill.

"Keep us moving," said Slocum, looking behind the coach. He saw nothing but the harsh emptiness stretching to the horizon. If he stood, Slocum thought he saw the promise of a storm in the hazy distance in the direction of the Rio Grande. But nowhere did he see riders. "Lose speed on this slope and the horses will have to strain getting back to their gait," snapped Slocum.

"Who's drivin' this here rig, Slocum? You or me?"

"Drive!"

Slocum didn't know what turned him so edgy. He saw no sign of horsemen riding down on them. The empty road ahead curled around between low hills larger than the stagecoach, but he saw no sign that they rode into an ambush. Still, Slocum couldn't chase away the uncomfortable feeling he was about to get his head blown off. He glanced at the iron express box at his feet and knew the powerful temptation there. If he hadn't hired on to protect the stagecoach, he'd be interested in appropriating this golden cargo.

But Slocum wasn't thinking of stealing the gold as much as guarding it. He had hired on to safeguard the passengers and freight on the Abilene Stage's huge, wallowing Concord coaches, and he'd see the job through to the best of his ability.

Even so, gold was a damnfool thing to die for, especially when it wasn't likely to ever be his. Slocum snorted at the thought of getting twenty dollars a trip for such duty, especially when he had to buy his own victuals along the way. About all three trips had gotten him was enough coin in his shirt pocket to buy the fancy new hat pulled down low on his forehead.

The stagecoach slowed as Doc Bond guided it between two towering rocks. Slocum's quick green eyes studied first the left boulder and then the right. His shotgun muzzle rose and his finger drew back on the double triggers without conscious thought. The first barrel discharged, and his finger kept curling back until the second barrel blasted forth its leaden death.

"What did you go and do that for?" Bond shouted. "You danged near deafened me." The driver stuck a gnarled finger in his ear and shook it, as if this might clear the ringing caused by the shotgun's discharge.

Slocum knocked open the breech and extracted the spent shells. He fumbled in his pocket for two more shells loaded with double–ought buck. Slocum didn't want to take any chances.

"Somebody was up there on top of the rock spying on us," Slocum said, turning around and laying the shotgun flat on the top of the stagecoach. He looked for a good target and never even caught sight of the man he'd fired on. It might have been a mirage, but Slocum didn't think so. The knot in his belly told him something powerful bad was about to happen.

"Didn't see nobody," Doc Bond grumbled.

"All I caught was the glint of sunlight off metal. Might have been a rifle barrel. Maybe it was a silver conch on an owlhoot's hat. Can't say since I didn't get good enough a sight. He must have been a lookout. If he didn't signal friends, then they'll still be alerted by the shotgun blast."

"Never thought you'd up and get nervy on me, Slocum. When I saw you in Abilene that first time, I said to myself that there's a young man with ice water in his veins. No, sir, never thought you'd get goosey on me and spook the horses."

"How far to the next depot?" Slocum wiped dirt from his face as he stared at the empty road behind them. He thought he caught sight of a small billow of brown dust. A dust devil whirling its way across the prairie or road agents coming after the stage? Slocum couldn't say.

"Maybe a couple miles. Old Jensen's the station master. You'll like him, Slocum. He's got stories about the war that will make your hair stand on—"

The bullet singing through the air missed by a country mile, but the sound brought Doc Bond up in the hard seat. He looked like a prairie dog getting ready to give the warning to others in his town. Bond's head swiveled first this way and then that, but he drew a blank as Slocum had done before.

The only thing the old driver couldn't deny now was the slug that had come sailing out of the empty prairie.

"What's goin' on, Slocum? Are we bein' robbed?"

"Reckon so, old timer," said Slocum. The dust cloud took form. It wasn't a tornado spinning around and kicking up dust. He made out at least three riders, maybe four. Slocum checked his pockets to see how many shells he had for the shotgun. Only eight. He dived under the seat and rummaged about for a spare box of shells. He knocked it open and frowned. What he had taken to be a full box held only six more shells.

He touched the Colt Navy hanging in its cross-draw holster and knew he had more ammo for the six-shooter in his bedroll—back in the boot with the passengers' baggage. It did no good there. He wished he had a long gun to keep the highwaymen at a distance, but his trusty Winchester was back in Abilene in a dingy hotel room.

"Get to the depot. We can't outgun them." From inside the coach Slocum heard loud cries of fright and indignation. The passengers weren't taking the sound of bullets winging past them too well.

Slocum leaned over and pushed aside a canvas curtain to peer at them. The two men had six-guns drawn. Slocum was glad they weren't so scared that they fired at any movement. He would have lost his face. His eyes drifted to the young woman riding in the rear. She sat, white-faced and obviously fighting to keep her fear under control.

"We've got a bit of trouble ahead of us," Slocum shouted to the men. The coach swayed crazily as Doc Bond's whipped the horses to their fastest pace. The team had tired over the rough road, and Slocum knew the horses would never maintain this clip for two miles, not dragging the heavy stagecoach. If the Abilene Stagecoach Company hadn't been so cheap, there would have been six strong horses instead of four broken down ones pulling the coach.

"Bandits?"

"Might be," Slocum said. "Don't worry too much about it. We'll be at the next depot in a few minutes. We'll be safe there." He saw relief flood over the woman's pale face. She gave him a weak smile that made Slocum feel like a complete scoundrel for lying. The two men knew what he really meant. They both spun the cylinders in their six-shooters and got ready for a fight.

The stagecoach rolled from side to side, and Slocum almost pitched off when Doc Bond took one curve in the road too fast. Slocum struggled to hang on, pulling himself back into the driver's box before they skidded in soft dirt around a second curve.

"The horses are tirin' out real quick on us," Bond called. He spat from the corner of his mouth without taking his eyes off the straining horses. Lather flecked the animals' heaving flanks. Slocum knew they would never reach the depot before the road agents overtook them.

He slid onto the top of the stagecoach and braced himself. It didn't take any skill using a scattergun, but he had to wait for the bandits to get into range. Again Slocum wished he had his rifle. He might not be able to hit any of the four men pursuing the coach, but with the Winchester he could keep them honest—for a spell.

Splinters flew up under Slocum's elbow, startling him. He rolled to his left side and saw two outlaws riding down hard on the coach from that direction. Swinging the scattergun around, he loosed a blast that deterred them for a few seconds. They got control of their frightened horses and came after the stagecoach again, six-guns firing. More wood exploded from the side of the stage. Slocum kept up a methodical firing with the shotgun until he hit one rider.

The man yelped and almost fell from the saddle. He

reined back, and Slocum knew he had only winged the outlaw. Worse, he had expended all but four of his shotgun shells.

"Don't fire until they get closer," Slocum yelled to the two men inside the stagecoach. "Don't waste your ammo."

He reared up and saw the four pursuing the stagecoach had narrowed the distance. They fired wildly, but occasional rounds came close enough to force Slocum back flat on the top of the stage.

"Doc, how far?" Slocum yelled. The outlaws would overtake them in a couple of minutes, and there wasn't a whale of a lot Slocum could do about it. Even if every shot from his six-shooter found a human target, that wouldn't be good enough. Two more road agents came at them from the right. Eight. And he had only five rounds in his Colt Navy and two more shotgun shells.

"The hell with it," Slocum said, firing the last rounds in the shotgun. He tossed it aside and rolled to his right to pull the keeper from the Colt's hammer. As he did, he saw Doc Bond turn and point. The depot lay ahead, less than a mile.

"Keep going," Slocum urged as he fumbled to get the leather thong off the six-gun's hammer.

"Don't worry your head none about that, boy," Doc Bond called back. "I'll—" Those were the driver's last words. A lucky shot caught him smack in the middle of his face. He half stood, then fell out of the driver's box without uttering another sound.

Slocum gripped the edge of the stage's roof and saw that Doc's body wasn't run over, not that it mattered much. The driver had been dead the instant the slug ripped into his head. Slocum scrambled forward, ducking the occasional slug coming his way. The outlaws weren't shooting accurately, but there were eight of them, and they carried a powerful lot of firepower, even if it was directed any which way.

Catching at the reins almost caused Slocum to take a serious spill. The leather straps slithered away, just out of his reach. He got his feet into the driver's box and tried again to take the reins. The horses ran wild now, the steady hand at their reins gone. Slocum swallowed hard and knew what he had to do if he wanted to keep everyone aboard the stagecoach from getting killed.

The depot came closer by the second, but the horses would thunder past it, and the outlaws would quickly overtake them. The only hope for survival that Slocum saw lay in the sanctuary offered by the adobe walls of the way station. The reins had fallen to the ground and threatened to tangle in the horses' hooves. The traces provided scant support for him to jump down onto the yoke and catch up the lines.

"Get ready for a crash," Slocum yelled to prepare the passengers for what had to come. Kicking hard, Slocum worked to knock free the linchpin holding the team to the stage. The horses' wild galloping made it dangerous, but Slocum succeeded. The pin popped free, separating the horses from the coach.

Slocum yelled as the stage overturned, sending him flying. He hit the ground hard and rolled into a clump of prickly pear cactus. The sharp spines caused him to recoil—and this saved his life.

Bullets dug into the thirsty ground where he would have been content to lie, stunned, if not for the thorns. Slocum got his feet under him and dragged out his six-gun. The Colt Navy belched fire once, twice, a third time. He felt scant satisfaction in seeing one road agent drop his six-shooter and clutch his belly.

There were seven others, and they all had blood in their eyes as they rushed on, firing as they came.

"Get to the depot," Slocum shouted, hobbling back toward the stagecoach. He wrenched open a door and helped one passenger climb free. The man was stunned but still clutched his six-shooter. Slocum turned him in the direction of the attacking outlaws.

"Fire. Keep firing till we're safe." Slocum heard the hammer fall on a spent round and cursed. The man had already emptied his weapon.

By this time the second man had pulled himself from the wreckage of the stagecoach. Slocum didn't have to tell him to start firing. The man tried to aim, but his hand shook uncontrollably. Every round he sent in the outlaws' direction went wide of its target.

But Slocum was more worried about the young woman still inside. He jumped onto the side of the over-turned stage and peered down into the coach. The dark–haired woman lay moaning, clutching her right arm. She turned bright blue eyes up at him imploringly. The outlaws were slowing their mad rush, but this only made their aim more deadly.

Slocum could join the two male passengers as they ran for the depot or he could try to pull the woman from the coach. Slocum never hesitated. He dropped beside her and tried to free her.

"What's caught?" he asked, finding she could not sit up. A few drops of blood showed where the woman had scratched herself, but her lack of movement came from some other cause.

"My dress is caught under the side of the coach," she gasped out. "Go on, save yourself. They won't do anything to me. I'm a woman."

Slocum almost laughed at her naïveté. Most men showed courtesy to a woman out West. But these men had already shown themselves to be killers. A simple barricade across the road would have stopped the coach, if robbery had been all that was on their minds. The outlaws thought nothing of riding up and filling the stagecoach full of holes. That meant they didn't intend to leave witnesses to their crime.

And a woman as lovely as the one struggling to pull her dress free from its entanglement wouldn't be killed right away. They might keep her for a few days or even a week before they tired of her.

"Here, let me get you out of that," Slocum said, yanking out his thick–bladed knife. The woman gasped, as if she thought he was going to cut her. He slashed savagely through her dress. The woman moaned but found she could sit up, freed from the tangling cloth.

"You ruined it," she said in a low, shocked voice.

"With any luck, you can get the Abilene Stagecoach Company to buy you a new one," Slocum said, hoisting himself out of the coach. A bullet almost took his hat off. He touched the brim of his new hat and found a bullet hole.

Cursing, he swung around and grabbed the woman, tugging hard. She lost a little more skin and a lot more of her full skirts, but Slocum got her onto the ground behind the stage.

"You run for the depot when I tell you," Slocum said.

"What are you going to do?" she asked, her blue eyes wide in horror at the sight of the outlaws shooting at them. Before she might have seen them as distant threats. Now she could almost smell their bad breath and see the bloodshot eyes. There was no escaping the knowledge these men would rather kill than spit.

Slocum moved around to the boot and cut away the straps holding the luggage in place. He found his bedroll. Safe within it was enough ammunition to hold off the road agents for a spell. He thrust the blanket into the woman's arms.

"Take this and get into the depot. The station master will cover you. So will the other two passengers." Slocum cast a quick look in the direction of the depot's open door. He saw an old man, nearly bent double with age, struggling to lift a buffalo rifle. The Sharps exploded as Slocum watched. The loud report as the .50 caliber slug cut through the air made his ears ring.

"Go on. Run. I'll keep them from gunning you down." Slocum wished he had time to unroll his blanket and get the spare ammo. He couldn't hope to hold off a full-scale attack if the seven remaining outlaws came for them all at once.

"Wait," the woman said. She gripped his arm and stared into the depths of his eyes. For a moment Slocum thought she was going to kiss him. Then she said, "Thank you," turned, and dashed off, seeking the safety of the depot. As she ran she clutched his blanket as if it meant her life.

Slocum smiled wryly. It might be just that important. Without ammunition, they would be at the outlaws' mercy—and Slocum doubted there was a speck of consideration in any of the owlhoots.

He fired with slow, methodical skill, taking out one highwayman's horse. The man shouted threats at Slocum as another of the outlaws picked him off the ground. Riding double, they rode out of range of Slocum's six-shooter.

Slocum cringed when the roar from the Sharps told of the station master's determination to join the fray. Six-shooter empty, Slocum knew he had to get to the adobe house or he'd end up buzzard bait. Judging distances, he turned and started to run. He skidded to a halt when he realized the outlaws had, for the moment, retreated to a safe distance. The strongbox gleamed in the hot Texas sun and drew Slocum powerfully. He had been hired to protect the passengers *and* the contents of that iron case.

Dropping to one knee, he spun about and grabbed the leather handles on either side of the heavy box. Grunting, Slocum pried the gold-laden container free from the driver's box. It crashed to the ground at his feet. Straining again, Slocum lifted the box to his shoulder and started for the stagecoach depot.

"Come on, man. Run. Forget the damned gold. Come

on now, you hear?'' The station master waved a gnarled hand in his direction, urging him to greater speed. Slocum felt like laughing. He had saved the passengers and, with a bit of luck, had also rescued the gold shipment. He had robbed the robbers!

He heard the distant pistol report but never felt the bullet that hit him in the back. John Slocum pitched forward onto the ground. His eyes fogged over and the world went from dusty brown to complete blackness.

2

Slocum shook his head and feared something had broken loose inside. Hornets buzzed about and turned his entire skull to liquid pain. The far–off sound of bullets reminded him of what had happened. He fought feebly, trying to keep his killers away. He heard distant voices, but he couldn't make out the words. His strength finally gave way, and he stopped fighting.

"About time," Slocum heard the rough voice in his ear. "Thought he'd never stop kicking."

New pain filled Slocum's world and forced him back to full consciousness. He blinked, stared straight ahead, and thought he had gone blind. Then he realized he was inside the dimly lit adobe house. Outside, six–shooters boomed like cannonade, reminding him of the years he had spent as sniper with the CSA. Some battles had sounded like hailstones hammering against a tin roof, bullets winging all around.

14

"Rip it away," he heard. Slocum fought to keep his mind on staying alive. He was inside the shelter of the thick–walled mud hut, but what had happened?

He stared up into the young woman passenger's bright blue eyes. She came over and ripped away his shirt. He winced as cloth tore part of his skin where blood had dried and matted fabric to his body.

"Feels bad," he told her. "Can't move my left arm."

"The bullet went plumb through your arm," the old station master said, peering over the woman's shoulder. "You up to tendin' him, little lady?"

"I am," she said primly. She set about probing the wound to be sure all fragments of the bullet were removed. Slocum passed out once, then came to. Nothing had changed. Gunfire told him the outlaws weren't giving up and taking their booty.

"I didn't get the express box," he said in a low voice. "Are the road agents still trying to kill us all?"

"It would seem so," the woman said. Her dark hair was mussed, but Slocum thought she looked like an angel. "Their greed knows no bounds. We—the other two passengers and I—cannot possibly have enough money and jewelry to make this assault worth their while."

Slocum said nothing to this. He had to agree. She had yet to consider what the attack really meant. By now the outlaws had stolen the depot's horses and anything in the stables worth taking. Since they hadn't hightailed it, they meant to kill all witnesses to their crimes. For them to go to such lengths meant they carried high rewards on their heads and didn't want the law knowing they were even in the area.

Or perhaps they were simply bloodthirsty killers. It hardly mattered what their motives were.

Slocum didn't have much truck with Texas Rangers, but he wouldn't mind seeing a company of them ride up about now. Instead of a ranger, a new hail of bullets filled the inside of the adobe house, shattering the frosted glass mantle of the coal oil lamp on the table. Slocum couldn't find much else inside the small adobe house that hadn't already been shot up.

"Them varmints ain't givin' up," the station master said. "Can't believe they gunned down Doc like that. He was 'bout my best friend." The old man shoved his long Sharps out the door and fired again. The recoil almost knocked him from his feet. Slocum would have offered to take over the chore of firing the powerful buffalo rifle except he could hardly sit up.

When he tried, the woman pushed him back down.

"You've lost too much blood, and you were right. Your left arm is broken. The bullet fragmented against the bone, and it was the devil's own work getting the pieces out."

"I'm much obliged," Slocum said. "Reckon I owe you my life."

"Hardly, sir," she said, smiling. "Rather, we owe you our lives. I am Ellen Garland and was on my way to Fort Griffin to—"

A new storm of lead cut off the explanation of why such a lovely woman traveled alone through central Texas in the middle of summer and a drought. Slocum groaned as he forced himself to sit up, despite Ellen's protests. He drew his six–shooter but found he could not load the gun one–handed. He looked up at her.

"The bedroll. My spare ammunition is in it. Can you load a percussion cap pistol?"

"I can learn," Ellen said gamely. She unrolled his blanket and pulled out the pouch of slugs and the rest of the fixings. Under Slocum's close scrutiny, she reloaded his Colt Navy.

Slocum took the time to lean against the cool adobe wall and muster his strength. They'd never get out of here alive if the outlaws decided to press their attack. The station master, Jensen, didn't have enough food and water inside for this many, and there was scant chance of escape if the highwaymen had stolen the Abilene Stagecoach Company's spare horses. Slocum wasn't too clear on how far it was from the depot on into Fort Griffin, but along the road it had to be at least twenty miles, maybe more. In this heat, that was a powerful long way to hoof it.

"Here," Ellen said, thrusting the six-shooter at him as if she had grabbed a rattler by the tail. Slocum took it and got to his feet just as one of the men passengers grunted and doubled over, folding like a bad poker hand.

"Don't bother with him," Jensen said. "He took it square in the heart. He was dead as a doornail 'fore he hit the floor." The old man fired the Sharps, staggered and sat down. Slocum started to laugh, then saw the red stain blossoming on the man's chest. He had been hit as he fired the powerful rifle.

"They're gonna kill us all," wailed the other passenger.

"Shut your mouth," snapped Slocum. He wasn't going to let the road agents kill him. If they wanted to leave him for the buzzards, they'd have to fight him every inch of the way to hell. "You panic and I guarantee we'll end up in graves."

"What do we do? They got more guns," the passenger said, trying to take hold of his fear. Slocum saw he was only partly successful. The man's eyes were wide and he panted hard. His pasty complexion told Slocum the man might keel over in a dead faint.

Glancing over his shoulder at Ellen Garland, he saw she held up much better. She was pale but composed. The set to her jaw and the way her lips thinned into a determined line told Slocum who he could depend on and who he couldn't. He reached down and picked up the dead passenger's fallen six-shooter.

"Use it," he said, handing it to Ellen. She took it in both hands, then moved to the window and cocked it. Slocum was glad that she pointed it outside. If the hog-

leg went off accidentally, at least the lead would go in
the right direction.

"What are you going to do? You got us into this
mess. You gotta get us out."

Slocum glared at the man. This wasn't anybody's
fault, except possibly for the owlhoots outside. But Slocum wasn't in any mood to argue.

"You're going to take the old man's rifle and cover
me. Fire until you run out of cartridges, then use your
six–shooter again."

"Where are you going? You gonna leave us?" The
man's voice turned shrill with fear. Slocum kept from
hitting him by strength of will. That would have forced
him to put down his Colt because his left arm hung limp
at his side, useless for a good fight. Instead, Slocum
clutched his six–shooter harder and fought to control
himself.

"I've got to see if there's any way we can drive them
off. Holing up in here won't do it. They've got us surrounded and can pot us like rabbits whenever we stick
our heads outside. If I can get *them* into a crossfire,
maybe they'll give up and leave."

"Think so?"

Slocum shrugged and regretted it. His shoulders were
aflame with pain. His discomfort brought Ellen Garland
from her post at the side window.

"Let me help," she offered. The woman quickly
bound his left against his side so it wouldn't flop
around when he ran. Slocum tried shifting his shoulders
again, but the pain proved too much. He bit down hard
and gritted his teeth.

"You cannot go out there," Ellen said. "You're in
no condition."

"I'm in better shape now than any of us will be unless
I try." Slocum saw that the other passenger firmed and
thrust the Sharps out the door. He triggered a round and
took a step back from the powerful recoil. Slocum nod-

ded, then ducked and raced along the outer wall of the
adobe house as the outlaws opened up on him. The passenger fired as fast as he could with the ungainly rifle,
but the road agents weren't having any of it. There
wasn't much danger to them.

Slocum saw two come out from behind bales of hay
stacked by the stables and straightforwardly shoot at
him. To Slocum's surprise, the report from a pistol came
from inside the adobe house and one outlaw grunted,
grabbing his leg.

"Ellen!" exulted Slocum. She was doing the work
the other passenger ought to, but Slocum didn't care
much who covered him. He kept low and dived behind
a watering trough. Slugs ripped into the wood, punctur-
ing it and causing some of the water to slowly drain.
Slocum used his new hat to get a drink before contin-
uing. The water refreshed him and gave more strength
than he would have thought possible.

Wiggling and keeping inches ahead of the bullets
seeking his body, Slocum came up behind a pile of
empty crates behind the adobe house. The wood boxes
gave scant protection. Now and then a bullet tore completely through the crates and made him flinch. Looking
around, he saw he couldn't stay there much longer. Already three of the road agents circled to get him in a
crossfire.

Slocum dug his toes into the dry ground and propelled
himself away from the crates and to a shallow irrigation
ditch running to a small garden. Flopping into it, Slocum
found a touch of mud at the bottom. He wasted no time
in slithering like a snake along the ditch until he came
up a dozen yards away.

Not ten paces away crouched one of the bandits, his
back to Slocum. Slocum wasn't above shooting the man
in the back, but he wanted to know who these owlhoots
were and why they were so intent on murdering everyone in the stagecoach depot. The notion fluttered across

Slocum's mind that the gold wasn't what these men really sought. They wanted somebody dead.

But who and why?

And was that only blowing smoke? Slocum knew men living by their wits, out in the wastelands, got mean and after a while took a joy out of killing for the sheer cruelty of it.

Slocum didn't have to shoot the man in the back. The outlaw turned and caught sight of him from the corner of his eye. The bandit whipped around his pistol and got off a quick shot that kicked up dirt in Slocum's face. Returning fire, Slocum knew he missed. Cursing, Slocum boiled from the ditch and went after the fleeing outlaw.

It was almost the last thing he ever did. Three others caught sight of him and opened fire. One bullet caught Slocum's boot heel and sent him tumbling. He landed hard on his broken left arm and almost passed out from the surge of pain blasting into his shoulder and brain. As much as the agony paralyzed him, it also saved his life.

If he had plunged on, he would have been killed. Realizing he could not stay on the ground any longer, Slocum rolled to the left, then rapidly reversed and rolled right. He gasped when a bullet's hot breath touched his cheek.

"The shotgun messenger's out behind the house!" The loud cry brought the sound of feet pounding hard on the ground. Slocum had only seconds before the outlaws swarmed on him like flies on fresh cow pies. He sat up and fired straight into the stables. Without a target, he shot only to keep the men at bay.

He was rewarded with a loud yelp of surprise and pain. He had winged another of the desperadoes, but he could not keep up this attack.

Every move made him a little woozier. Realizing his mission was foolhardy at best, he rolled back and kept going to avoid the bullets thumping into the dirt all around him. Ducking and dodging, Slocum made his way back to the adobe's open door.

The Sharps blasted just above his head. Slocum flung himself flat on the floor and yelled, "Watch out. It's me! Don't shoot me!"

"Sorry," came Ellen's trembling voice. She came to the door and grabbed his belt. Tugging hard, she dragged him into the adobe.

"You fire the buffalo gun?" he asked the young woman. Her head bobbed up and down as if it had been put on a spring.

He saw why she struggled with the heavy rifle. Sprawled flat on his back, arms outstretched lay the second male passenger from the stagecoach. The outlaws had reduced the number on the stage until only Slocum and Ellen Garland remained.

"You know any of the men outside?" he asked, still wondering if their tenacity rested on revenge rather than lust for gold.

"What?" The idea startled her. He saw Ellen wasn't likely to know men such as those.

"Nothing. I was thinking maybe they want something more from us. They might be powerful horny after being out on the lonesome prairie," he said, letting her absorb what he was saying, "but I doubt it. They opened fire early on and haven't given up."

"Might be they are just vicious killers," Ellen said.

Slocum had to agree. Still, he had to consider every angle. He dragged the dead men inside the adobe to the door and formed a small barricade with their bodies. He made sure the gunmen outside could see the faces.

"If they've got a feud going with any of these men, this ought to show they've reached their goal." Slocum knew nobody hunted him. He took a deep breath as he mentally amended that. He had any number of lawmen after him for past misdeeds.

After being gutshot and left for dead by Bloody Bill Anderson after the Lawrence, Kansas, raid during the war, Slocum had spent long months recovering, only to return home to find Slocum's Stand abandoned. His parents had died months earlier. Slocum had tried to make a success of the family's farm in Calhoun, Georgia, but a carpetbagger judge had other ideas.

No taxes had been paid, the judge said, eyeing Slocum's Stand for a stud farm. "Evicted," the judge had said, riding out with a hired gun to throw Slocum off land that had been in his family since George I had given it to his ancestors before the Revolutionary War.

"Dead," said Slocum, cutting down both the judge and his gunman after a fair fight. He had been running ever since, with a warrant for judge–killing dogging his steps.

If that had been all that was in Slocum's past, he might have found a place to light. Trouble followed him as if he were a lightning rod, and for the most part, Slocum reveled in it. But right now, he was in a quiet portion of his life. Nobody wanted his scalp.

"You don't know them, and neither do I," said Slocum, peering out the door into the late afternoon sun. The heat worked for him right now. The outlaws were in the sun and he and Ellen were in the coolness of the thick–walled house. "Let's hope they see a face they're after and let us be."

More bullets put this to the lie. Slocum knew the gunmen outside could see that only two of them remained. If the killing kept on, that meant the road agents wanted to make their slaughter complete. They weren't out to settle a feud. They were out to see blood, and it didn't matter whose.

"What are we going to do, John?" Ellen asked. She dropped the heavy rifle and spread her hands. He didn't have to be told the buffalo rifle was useless without any more ammunition.

"We can try to make a run for it," he said, considering their chances. Slocum didn't think they stood too good a chance. He took a look at the watering trough, his mouth dry again. The taste of water when he dodged outside the first time had only whetted his thirst, not slaked it.

"I am not sure I can keep up. I would be a handicap for you, John. You go. I'll cover you again."

"And?" he pressed her. "What if I do get away? What should I do? I don't have enough ammunition to kill all of them, even if they lined up and let me take a shot at each in turn."

"Why, go get help. Fort Griffin—"

"Is twenty miles by road. I make it out to be about twelve miles if we cut across yonder ridge," Slocum said, pointing to the northeast. "It would be morning before I could get back with a posse, even if I could interest the town marshal in riding out."

"The cavalry post," she said in a small voice. "They would come out here."

"Probably," Slocum said, remembering the lost military payroll. "More likely, they'd string me up for losing their pay." He settled down and fired a few times to let the outlaws know they weren't giving up. "Do you think you could hold them off for twelve hours?"

"Why, if I had to," Ellen said. Slocum had to admire her pluck, even if she didn't have any idea what she would face.

"Even if you stayed awake, they could sneak up on you when it got dark." He studied the setting sun through a side window that was hardly more than a slit in the thick adobe.

"Surely, Shackleford County has a sheriff willing to enforce the law," Ellen said disdainfully. She saw his surprise. "I am not a complete babe in the woods, sir. I am aware of geography and other matters. I was born and raised down in Austin."

"So you know all the counties in Texas," Slocum said. "That doesn't do much to get us away."

"Your attitude is not helping, John," she said, softening her tone. "I know you are doing your best, but it looks hopeless, doesn't it?"

"I'm afraid it does," Slocum said, fresh out of ideas. "They must be getting hot and tired in the sun. Might be we can get away when it gets a little darker."

Slocum hunched down and peered into the dying light. He knew they could never hope to get away facing eight muzzles and a lot of meanness. Staying in the house, though, was a one-way ticket to death. With Ellen's help, he reloaded his Colt Navy, seeing that this was the last of his ammunition.

Ellen Garland saw this, too.

"We have to do something quickly, John. I'm ready to run for it, if you are. Where do we go?"

"Head for the stables out back. We can find a place to hide and then find some horses." He hadn't seen any mounts in the stable. The outlaws had already taken them. Then Slocum found himself completely occupied with just staying alive. The robbers charged, their six-shooters blazing.

Slocum fired six times until his hammer fell on an empty cylinder. He turned and looked forlornly at Ellen Garland. He didn't have to tell her this was the end. With a broken arm and no ammunition, there was no way he could fight off the outlaws.

3

"They'll be coming for us soon, won't they, John?" Ellen Garland fought to hold back tears. Slocum stared out the door, searching the lengthening shadows for movement. He didn't bother telling her how right she was. The outlaws had to know their victims were out of ammunition. A few quick rounds sent into the adobe house with no shots in reply would convince them of that. Slocum's thumb flicked against the hammer of his useless Colt Navy.

Even if he had all the ammo in the world, he knew their position was indefensible. He had been in enough shoot–outs to recognize when he could win and when it was time to die. The only thing was, John Slocum wasn't the kind to give up. Ever.

"We can't get out of here without them spotting us," he told Ellen. She broke out sobbing and came to him. Her face buried into his shoulder. Her tears soaked into

25

his shirt. Slocum wished he could save just a fraction of that moisture for drinking. His throat was parched. The Texas sun had scorched the land all day. Even inside the cool adobe house, it had been brutal.

"So hot," he muttered, his arms around the woman's quaking shoulders. The kernel of an idea came to him. He pushed Ellen away and looked into her tear–filled eyes. "You willing to take a big risk?"

"W–will it save us?" She couldn't help looking at the bodies in the doorway. Slocum doubted she knew either of the passengers. Ellen certainly hadn't known the old galoot running the stagecoach way station. Slocum had come on this route twice before and he wouldn't have recognized the driver's good friend away from the depot.

"We're going to die if we don't try something. This is desperate, but it might keep us alive a spell longer."

"What do we have to do?" Ellen glanced past him to the cool shadows outside. "I can't run very fast. And in these skirts . . ." She turned slightly from side to side to show how constricting the fancy skirt she wore would be.

"No running," Slocum said. The outlaws had already stolen the horses. Without sturdy mounts and a share of water, he and Ellen stood no chance at all against their attackers. "We're going to try something more dangerous."

"What? How could anything be more dangerous?" Ellen asked, eyes widening in surprise. The notion intrigued her that dashing out of the adobe with the bandits shooting at them was less risky than anything else he might propose.

"See that trench near the back wall?" Slocum pointed to a shallow ditch the station master had dug for some reason all his own. It ran the length of the back wall and was less than a foot deep. "Maybe the old gent was going to put up a second wall to keep out the heat. That side faces south. Or maybe he was burying his money. It doesn't matter much now.''

''A furrow such as that one cannot possibly help us,'' she said, frowning now. For a moment she had been caught up in the thrill of escape. Not seeing the extent of Slocum's plan, she had given up. ''I doubt we could tunnel under the mud brick wall quickly. And what would that gain us?''

''Not a thing,'' Slocum said. He found a pickax and a shovel in the far corner where the station master had left them. Hefting them, Slocum began working feverishly, if awkwardly because of his broken arm. There wasn't much time before the outlaws rushed them ''Take up the Sharps and poke it out the door now and again. Keep them thinking you're looking for a good target— and let me know if you see the whole passel of them coming in for us.''

''John, tell me what you're doing.''

''You wouldn't take kindly to it,'' Slocum said, applying himself with vigor to the task of deepening the trench. Clumsily using the pick in one hand, he scraped and twisted as much as he swung. Using the shovel proved a little easier, but not much. Every move he made sent new waves of pain through his broken arm. Worse, the ground proved hard going and he gave up when he hit a layer of caliche. Getting through the white, sun-baked, claylike material would take more work than he wanted to expend right now. Speed counted for more than depth, he hoped. Lengthening the ditch, he dug it down a full eighteen inches. Then he poked straight through the back wall until he had made a hole the size of his hand just above ground level. Through the hole he saw only dusty ground.

''Any sign of them getting antsy?'' Slocum tossed down the shovel and stared at his handiwork. The cut ran the length of the back wall, some ten feet. He hadn't bothered widening it, but the foot–and–a–half depth would have to be sufficient.

"I'm not sure. I don't know what to watch for," Ellen answered honestly. "John, I'm frightened. I was scared before, but now it's really getting to me."

He knew what she was going through. At first, the woman had recognized intellectually that she might die. Now the emotional impact of it was coming home to roost. This fear might freeze her up at a critical instant. Slocum knew he had to keep her busy doing things that had to get finished and preventing her from thinking of the desperadoes outside.

"Break up the table," he told her. "Get the planks free. At least two of them," he said, judging distances. "It's about time for me to get us free." He grabbed up his blanket and the one off the station master's bed and stuffed them under his broken arm. He went to the door and chanced a quick look out. The outlaws were beginning to come for them. It was time.

"John, wait!"

Slocum rolled over the bodies forming the barricade in the door and immediately became the target for a half dozen angry slugs winging his way. He jerked when one brushed his broken arm. This gave him the reason to move faster. He rose up near the water trough and crashed down inside it. Rolling over and over in the shallow water remaining, he thoroughly soaked himself. When he was sure he had drenched the blankets, also, he turned over the back edge of the trough and hit the ground. New rounds sought his flesh as he dashed back inside.

"John, what was that all about? You're soaked!"

"In the trench," he said, shoving Ellen toward the south wall. She stumbled and fell. He kept pushing her until she lay in the channel. He covered her with one of the soaked blankets, then put part of the table over her. He began shoveling dirt atop her.

"What are you doing?" she cried. "Don't bury me alive!"

"Shut up and trust me. I'll be joining you in a few minutes." Slocum wobbled from pain as he got a few inches of dirt atop the wood plank over Ellen's body. He created an air hole for her by digging a shallow ditch to meet the hole through the foot–thick adobe. Breeze from the cooling twilight gusted into her face.

Not wasting a moment, Slocum got the bottle of coal oil meant for the shattered lamp and doused it over everything he could find in the house. He made sure the bodies in the doorway were especially soaked. Then Slocum fumbled out a lucifer and lit it. The flare instantly ignited the volatile lamp oil. He rolled quick as a fox to the trench and put his head down next to Ellen. Working in the constrained space, he pulled the other waterlogged blanket over his body and placed the second plank from the table across his legs. Sitting up, he began shoving as much of the remaining dirt from his digging over the wood as possible.

"John, the heat! It's horrible," moaned Ellen. He didn't stop to reassure her. He got only a thin layer over his planking before the heat forced him low.

With their faces just inches apart, Slocum pulled up the wet blanket until their heads were covered. Breathing proved difficult; he hadn't cut a big enough hole through to the outside. And within the house the fire blazed ever higher.

"Don't panic," he told her. "If we're lucky, the fire will destroy everything inside the depot."

"Will they think we were killed?"

"I hope so. There's no telling what they might do. Unless I miss my bet, they won't want to sift through the ashes to find our corpses." Slocum almost gagged as the smell of burning flesh reached his nostrils. The other bodies stacked in the doorway provided an even greater barrier against the outlaws now. If the road agents came close to the doorway, the choking scent would drive them off.

Or so Slocum hoped.

"John, this is awful," Ellen said, beginning to cry again.

On impulse, Slocum bent over the inch separating them and kissed her gently on the forehead. It was all he could do in the tight confines of the ditch he had dug. Or was it their grave? He hoped he would be able to sit around one day and think on the subject and decide it was a clever stunt. Right now, he wasn't so sure he had done the right thing.

The heat rose and burned at him, even through the feeble barriers of dirt and wood and wet blankets he had wrapped them in. Slocum tried to keep from moaning as pain in his arm worsened. Concentrating on breathing slowly, he craned his head about to catch any fresh air from outside. There was damned little.

Some time during the firestorm ravishing the adobe house, Slocum passed out from pain and lack of air.

"John! John!"

Slocum moaned and tried to shake himself awake. He was tightly bound and unable to move. His eyes flickered open and the pieces began to fit together again. He remembered what he had done.

"What is it?" he asked Ellen. "The fire's out. I don't feel the heat anymore."

"They're coming in after us!"

"Shush," he soothed, still fighting the pain in his arm and body. Parts of his legs had blistered from the heat. He knew the woman might not be in any better condition, though he had tried to put her in the deeper section of the trench and had insulated her body with a few more inches of dirt.

Rising up, Slocum pushed back the blanket that had protected his face. He was in a better position to see

than Ellen Garland. The outlaws came into the smoldering interior, guns drawn.

"Quiet," he cautioned. "Play dead."

"Won't be hard," she whispered back. "I feel as if
I'm almost there."

Slocum blinked back dirt from his eyes as he watched
the two gunmen enter. They both carried six–shooters,
cocked and ready for action. One stepped over the sim-
mering mess of dead bodies at the door and came into
the house. The other made gagging sounds and turned
to stick his head outside.

"Don't go doin' that," complained the man in the
house, but Slocum saw he wasn't being too manly about
poking through the charred remains inside. The outlaw
pulled up his bandanna and made only a cursory examination of the house before leaving. From outside the
door, Slocum heard their faint voices.

"Reckon the fire got 'em both," the more adventur-
ous of the pair said. "That takes care of any witnesses."

"I don't see why we had to wait around," complained
the second. "They couldn't identify us."

"You know what the boss said. We don't take no
chances. Everybody's got to die when we rob a stage.
Makes it harder for the law to pin anything on us if they
ever catch us."

"Hell, the pea–wits in these parts can't touch the likes
of us," boasted the second man, his bravado returning
now that he was out of the smoldering adobe house.
"We're too smart for any lawman."

"Let's tell the boss we done what he wanted," said
the first. Slocum thought the soft whispering noise he
heard might be a six–shooter returning to its holster.

"Yeah, and then we can divvy up the gold. I've
worked up a powerful thirst. My share'll go for a few
bottles of good whiskey and a woman. Two! I'll have
enough for *two* women."

"You're so damned ugly, there ain't that much money

in the world for you to buy two,'' joked the first. Their footfalls receded and Slocum relaxed, collapsing back into the trench.

"We're safe," he said, barely daring to speak. "We'll have to wait a spell for them to get on out of here, but they're not looking for us any longer."

"They thought we'd died?"

Slocum dropped his head on the dirt just an inch away from Ellen's face and tried to answer. All strength left him again and he passed out.

Cool water splashed against his face. Slocum sputtered and ran his good hand over it, wiping some of it onto his parched lips. He didn't want to open his eyes and find that he had died. He just wanted to lie in the coolness and let the breezes blow around him.

That thought caused him to sit bolt upright. Waves of pain shot through him but the pain focused his attention. He lay outside under the stars. Only in the Texas prairie were the stars so clear and close. He wondered if he reached out if he could touch them. Then his brain cleared even more.

"Ellen?"

"Right here, John. I wanted out of that grave so badly, but I waited. How I waited!"

"How long?"

"Hours. I saw the last of the light vanish and only when the moon came up did I venture out. I listened real hard for the outlaws, but they must have gone right after those two checked the house."

"Might have. Nothing here to hold them. They'd taken everything of value." Slocum eagerly splashed more water on his face as Ellen put down a water bucket beside him. Using his good hand, he scooped up water and drank his fill. Only when he worried he might start to bloat like a horse, did he slow. Then he ran his damp fingers through his long, lank black hair. He was sadly in need of a bath and tending, but those lay a far piece off.

"They rode west, toward the Rio Grande. Do you think they're going into Mexico to avoid the law?"

Slocum laughed harshly. "What are they running from? Nobody knows who they were. Those bush-whackers were too thorough. I couldn't identify a one of them. And they killed everyone else."

"I can't testify against them," Ellen said in a small voice. "I never saw any of them."

"So they got away scot–free," Slocum said, anger tingeing his words. He wanted each and every one of those backshooters in his sights, and he knew it would never happen. They would ride off with their spoils, and he could belly up to a bar next to them and not know.

He pushed revenge from his mind and turned to something more immediate: survival.

"We can't stay here," he said, coming to a quick decision. Even as he'd been out dodging bullets earlier, a plan had been taking shape in his head. Staying at the depot wouldn't do them much good since the next stage-coach from Abilene wouldn't be along for well nigh a week. There wasn't much left inside the house to eat, and Slocum knew he couldn't trap and hunt for anything with a busted wing.

"No ammunition," Ellen pointed out. "And I've al-ready searched for food. There isn't any. What was stored out back, the outlaws took."

"That and the horses might have been what they were after. Leastwise, we have a few drops of water."

"I got the burlap bag from the coach," she said. "I filled it. It's surprising how cool the water gets inside."

"Evaporation cools it down," Slocum said. Desert bags were good for short stretches, but they didn't hold water worth beans. The leakage would do them in unless they walked at night—and fast.

"What are we going to do without horses?" The

woman began rinsing off Slocum's face. At first he tried
to push her away, then relented. It felt mighty good letting such a lovely woman clean him up.

"Walk. Fort Griffin is a ways northeast across the
prairie, but we can make it if we start right away." Slocum tried to figure out what time it was by the stars.
The best he could determine, it was a tad past midnight.
He tried to pull out his brother's watch, but his fingers
wouldn't work right. Ellen gently pushed him flat onto
the blanket she'd laid out.

"Don't worry about that right now. Rest. We've both
been through hell." She rose up beside him and stared
down with adoring eyes. "John, you saved my life. How
can I ever thank you?"

"I saved both our hides," he said. "It wasn't anything."

"It was. I've never had anyone do for me what you
just did." Ellen sank down beside him, her nimble hands
working to unfasten his trousers. He tried to push her
away, but she adamantly refused.

"I want this, John. If you're able, I want this."

"Can't move too much, and my left arm's no good."

"Then lie back and let me do it all." Ellen began
working him free of his seared clothing. Slocum helped
the best he could, wondering if he was in any shape for
what Ellen so obviously wanted. When he felt her fingers circle his manhood, he experienced small twinges
deep inside. As she stroked, he responded fully.

"Didn't think that was going to happen," he said as
she continued to slip gently along him. Then her hand
tightened around the firm shaft and worked even harder.
Slocum moaned and lay back, closing his eyes. The sensations rippled through him and made him tingle all
over.

For the first time in longer than he could remember,
there were more good feelings than bad rattling around
in his body. He gasped when he felt wetness circle the

tip of his lust–hardened length. He opened his eyes and lifted up enough to see Ellen's lips close around him.

Her tongue danced all over him, and new thrilling sensations rippled into his loins. His hips began a little dance as he thrust up, trying to get even more into her mouth. Ellen backed off and gently chided him.

"That's not what I want, and I don't think it's all you want."

"No, no it's not," he said as the woman opened her blouse to expose a tangled, dirty array of once fine, frilly undergarments. Ellen ripped them free. Her large, luscious breasts tumbled out, turned to silver in the bright Texas moonlight. Slocum reached up with his right hand and gently tweaked one nipple.

Ellen leaned back, closed her eyes, and purred like a kitten with a bowl of cream. She wiggled from side to side, mashing herself down more firmly into Slocum's grip.

"Harder, John. Do it harder. It sets me on fire inside."

He didn't know how hard to twist and turn and tweak, but nothing he did seemed enough to satisfy her. She hiked her skirts and straddled his waist. Slocum immediately found himself buried balls deep in a tight, damp tunnel of desire. Ellen turned from side to side, as if she could take him even deeper into her body.

"You're turning me inside out," moaned Slocum. He reached up and cupped her breast, pushing her upward.

"You want more?" she taunted. "How much more?"

"More!" he gasped out. She did things to him without using her hands. The sheath so snugly gripping his length tensed and stroked and repeated all her hand had accomplished earlier. Then she lifted her weight slightly off his hips. He slid from her and desired nothing else but to be back in.

"Now?" Ellen dropped down, crashing hard into his groin. The feelings built within as Slocum tried to hold back the fiery flood of his seed. He didn't want this to

end, and it had just started. He wasn't any anxious teen-
age buck with his first woman. He had been with so
many women he couldn't rightly remember all of them,
but none had been as pretty as Ellen—or as eager to
please.

Wiggling her hips from side to side, she corkscrewed
her way up and down. His heart pounded fiercely and
made his iron–hard manhood twitch. This excited the
woman even more. He felt as if he had pushed into a
warm tunnel and the walls had collapsed around him.
Ellen began rising and falling faster. The friction of their
contact burned at him, searing his flesh and igniting his
passions.

He tried to control the way Ellen rose and fell by
gripping her breasts. He couldn't do it. She was too lost
in the wilderness of her own emotions to notice what he
did. If anything, his clumsy groping only spurred her on.
She rose and fell faster and faster, moaning every time
she slid down his full length.

"John, so big, you're so big! Can't get enough."

Slocum stared up at the bright stars, then closed his
eyes and let the waves of desire wash over him. He
couldn't do much to help her, so he simply took what
Ellen offered so freely. His balls tightened and then
erupted, spilling forth their creamy white cargo.

Ellen Garland sobbed out something he didn't hear
too clearly, arched her back, and then went wild. Her
body shook all over as she lifted and fell on his length.

Then she bent forward, her sweating head pressed into
his shoulder again. He felt hot breath gusting across his
chest. The woman cried softly.

"There's nothing to be sorry for," he tried to console
her. "We've been through so much—"

"You don't understand, John." Ellen pushed up and
looked down at him. The tears still ran down her cheeks
leaving muddy tracks, but a wicked little smile crossed

her ruby lips. "I wanted to do this. It's on my head, not yours."

"I wasn't objecting," he said, not sure what thoughts ran through the lovely, dark-haired woman's head. Women were always a mystery, and Ellen was no different from any other—just prettier and braver.

"It's a long way to Fort Griffin, even if we cut across the prairie, isn't it?" she said, changing the subject so fast on him it took a couple seconds for the words to soak in.

"It's a good twelve miles. And it's only about six hours until sunrise. We ought to be able to make it before the heat wears us down overmuch."

"Then let's stop talking and get moving," Ellen Garland said, standing. Slocum looked up and saw the lusciously naked breasts and the gorgeous face. For her he would walk through hell on broken glass.

But he found it almost more than he could bear to just sit up. It was going to be a very long walk into town.

4

"We should wait awhile, John. You're in no condition to go on." Ellen Garland's worried voice cut through the haze of white–hot pain wrapped around Slocum like a heavy, suffocating blanket. He shook his head and tried to tell her he was all right. The words got all jumbled in his throat.

He coughed, sat on the rocky ground, and stared up at the stars, trying to figure how long they had been walking. The constellations swung around in unfamiliar patterns, as if he had been dropped on the other side of the world.

"We've been walking almost three hours, John. I don't get the feeling we're going anywhere."

"We're making progress," he assured the lovely woman. "We're getting there." In the darkness, her pale face seemed to glow from an inner light. The moon had set long ago, and that gave him some vague reason to worry. It had been only a six–hour walk to Fort Griffin from the burned–out way station. He tried to get his bearings from the North Star and found it hard because his mind wandered so.

Slocum couldn't tear his eyes off the Big Dipper. Water. The promise of cool, soothing liquid trickling down his throat. He coughed again and wondered if the black gob carried blood with it. Slocum had been shot up and his arm hurt like a thousand red ants had taken up residence in his joints. Worst of all was the way his chest hurt. He hadn't been hit in the body by any of the road agents' flying lead, but that was cold comfort. Being battered and beaten, shot up, and going through the fire he'd set inside the adobe depot had all taken a great toll on his strength.

"John," he heard Ellen say from far away. Then he realized she was shaking him gently.

"Hurts," he grumbled. "Don't do that." Visions flashed through his mind that confused him. He remembered the depot fire and the bullets and their lovemaking. That was about the only good memory he had of being shotgun messenger for Abilene Stagecoach Company. He had lost the gold–laden strongbox holding a payroll for the troopers at the fort. Nobody would cotton to that.

The cavalry would think it was his fault that the road agents had taken their gold. The stagecoach company would know it was. They'd hired him, and he had failed to protect their property. They might even get their dander up over Doc Bond and the station master being killed. Slocum doubted they would much care that two passengers had also died. They had already paid for their tickets.

"John," Ellen said more insistently. "I'm tired from walking, and I think we're going in a big circle. I'm not sure we haven't come back to the depot."

"Couldn't have," he said, shaking his head. This cleared his vision and thoughts a mite. He got to his feet and looked around. Getting bearings at night in the middle of the prairie wasn't as easy as he'd thought it would be. Slocum had spent most of his life in the wilderness tracking and hunting. He ought to have been in Fort Griffin by now and couldn't explain why he wasn't enjoying a warm bath and a soft bed in a fine hotel.

"Which way do we go?" Ellen Garland's voice carried more than a hint of exasperation with him. He wobbled to his feet and set out with long strides that quickly weakened.

"You simply cannot go on any longer," Ellen said. "Don't be a fool, John."

"I'm not. We have to walk *tonight*." He knew that they would die in the summer heat if the sun rose and they hadn't found shelter. The best chance they had of getting away from the scorpions and rattlers and other deadly life Doc Bond had warned of lay in reaching Fort Griffin.

"We can find shade somewhere and sit out the day while you rest," the lovely, dark–haired woman insisted. She moved closer to him and laced her arm through his, offering some measure of support. Slocum gratefully accepted. Each step he took tired him that much more.

He kept looking up at the sky to get his bearings and every time, the stars moved. Once, he fished out his pocket watch and peered at the face. He hardly believed it. Four hours. Four hours they had been stumbling across the prairie. By now they ought to have reached the outskirts of Fort Griffin. It wasn't much of a town, but the outlying houses would give them as much chance for survival as the town itself.

He hadn't seen even a cavalry patrol.

"Something's wrong, isn't it?" Ellen wouldn't be put off any longer. "We're lost. We have been walking in a circle."

"No, no," he denied. He thought he was getting a mite feverish. The cold wind whipping across the prairie chilled him something fierce. He pulled his blanket tighter around his shoulders and found no comforting warmth in it.

"We've come in a wide circle, and this is the road to Fort Griffin." Ellen stamped a small foot, making Slocum look at the ground. To his surprise, they had blundered across a road.

"But it's twenty miles by road. It should have been only twelve the way we were going." Slocum didn't understand how he could have gone this wrong. He was a good tracker and could find his way out of any predicament.

"We sit, you rest," Ellen ordered in a firm, indignant voice. She shoved him to the ground. He tripped and fell heavily. Pain rocketed through him from his injured shoulder. All he could do was groan and pass out.

Slocum experienced the next few hours in fits and starts. The sun rising and burning down on him. Water trickling across his lips. Ellen's soothing voice. Fitful catnaps followed by periods when he sat up and looked around, not really seeing anything. And then came distant thunder. He tried to tell her the danger of going into gullies. The rains filled the arroyos and turned them into drowning pools in a flash. But the words wouldn't come.

He heard Ellen shouting and moving away from him. He wanted her to stay close if it was going to rain. Texas storms were unpredictable and vicious. Real frog stranglers. Then the thunder went away and silhouettes moved between him and the sun, casting momentary shade.

"Hello," he said, reaching out to shake hands. He was hoisted up easily and dropped as if he were only a small child's toy. Slocum lay full length and only after an hour of bouncing along did he come to his senses. He grabbed for his six-shooter, remembering too late that it was empty.

"Calm yourself, John," Ellen said, sitting beside him

in the wagon bed. "Mr. Beals was kind enough to give us a ride into Fort Griffin. He just happened along the road."

"Found the depot and pushed my team so's I could report the massacre," Beals said from the driver's box. "Knew something bad had happened. Thought it might have been Comanches because of the way everybody'd died. They've been on the warpath for months now. Didn't reckon it to be highwaymen."

"Eight of them," Slocum croaked out. "Winged a couple, but not too bad."

"You ended up on the short end of the fight, from the way you look. Miz Garland took real good care of you. If she hadn't, you'd be plumb dead by now. Yes, sir." Beals turned and tended to his driving. Slocum drifted in and out of sleep, sitting up only when he heard the bustle of a town around him. Forcing himself up using the edge of the wagon for support, he saw the small town of Fort Griffin—The Flats, the locals called it to distinguish it from the cavalry post a mile farther down the road.

"I told Mr. Beals to drop us off in front of the doctor's office."

"No, wait, got to tell the stagecoach manager about the robbery," Slocum protested. He felt responsible for all that had happened. He didn't know how he could have held off eight armed and determined road agents, but he had been hired to do just that. Men had died, two Abilene Stagecoach Company employees and two passengers. That had to be reported to the manager and the town marshal.

"The doctor, Mr. Beals," Ellen insisted. "If you would inform the sheriff of our problem, it would be greatly appreciated."

"Be glad to, Miz Garland," the rancher answered, touching the tip of his Stetson in acknowledgment. The wagon rumbled along for a few more blocks and then creaked to a halt outside a woman's clothing store.

"Dr. Woodson's upstairs, round back. Need any help getting him out?"

Slocum realized for the first time Beals spoke only to Ellen and not to him. He tried to reply angrily and found the words choking him. He needed more water, and he wished it wasn't so damned hot. Even with the blanket over him, though, he shuddered. Nothing made much sense.

Beals and Ellen got him from the wagon and led him around to the rear. The stairs leading to the upstairs office were almost more than Slocum could negotiate. He struggled up the last step and Ellen opened the door. He fell through onto the doctor's floor.

"I do declare, folks are just dyin' to see me," came a jovial response to Slocum lying facedown on the floor.

"He's badly hurt. His left arm is broken, and he is running a fever," Ellen stated in her precise manner. "Can you help him?"

"If'n he don't up and die on me first. But don't you worry your pretty head none about that, miss. My brother–in–law's the town undertaker. We can give you good rates."

Slocum was in no mood for the doctor's humor. Surprisingly strong hands lifted him and gently placed him on an examination table. He got his first glimpse of the doctor and thought he had been mysteriously transported to the northern timberlands. Towering above him was a bearded man who looked more like a lumberjack than a doctor. He was even dressed in a plaid shirt rather than the more formal white shirt and cravat sported by most doctors.

"You ought to read medicine," Dr. Woodson said, pulling away Slocum's blood–soaked sleeve. "You gave a concise and accurate diagnosis. This here arm's busted to hell and gone, but I kin fix it right up."

Slocum passed out after being given a stiff slug of

whiskey. When he woke up, the shadows stretched across the room. Ellen Garland sat in a chair beside him, reading a small Bible. She glanced up when she felt his eyes on her. Ellen smiled and Slocum felt worlds better.

"Dr. Woodson said you would be coming around about now. He is a very good doctor."

"Not feeling much pain," Slocum said, surprised at the way the doctor had patched him up. He tried moving his left arm and experienced a passing twinge. Other than this, he had left behind the constant agony assailing him.

"I'm not sure what he gave you, but it must have been powerful medicine." Ellen closed her Bible and slipped it away in the folds of her dress. Slocum saw she had bought a new dress. It was simple and plain, but the woman's beauty overshadowed whatever clothing she might wear.

Slocum saw the empty whiskey bottle on the doctor's desk and knew the warm glow in his belly came from its depths. "The doctor *is* a good one," he admitted. "How much is he charging for this?" He lifted his left arm and saw that it was completely wrapped in tight bandages. He wouldn't be getting into any fights for quite a spell.

"He said it would be twenty dollars. He did a considerable amount of work setting your arm."

Slocum touched his vest pocket. He had three crumpled greenbacks resting there. No more. For a fleeting moment, he wondered if Ellen might have any money, then pushed it from his mind. He was already beholden to her for all she had done. Saving his life had required quite a bit of tenacity out on the prairie, what with his broken arm and his head all twisted up with fever.

"I can't pay him. You reckon he might take my IOU?"

"They're quite hospitable here in Fort Griffin," Ellen said. "He might do that very thing. I was given this dress by the wife of the pastor.''

"You get the Bible from her, too?''

"From the pastor himself,'' Ellen said, smiling almost shyly. ''It's been a long time since I read the Scriptures.''

Slocum swung his feet over the edge of the table and discovered some measure of strength had returned. He walked slowly to the door, gaining stamina with every step. He wasn't up to tangling with a bucking bronco or spending twenty hours in the saddle chasing down strays on a roundup, but he wasn't bedridden as he had feared.

He heard heavy footsteps coming up the stairs. He opened the door, thinking to speak to Dr. Woodson about the bill. Instead of the brawny doctor, Slocum faced a whip–thin man with huge mustaches. The seven–pointed star on his vest told his occupation.

"You're Slocum,'' the lawman said without preamble. ''McGrath tole me all about you and how you upped and lost the gold shipment.''

"I didn't exactly lose it, marshal,'' Slocum said. ''There was a powerful lot of shooting that went ahead of the gold being stolen by a gang of eight road agents.''

"McGrath says there'll be hell to pay when Captain Stanley over at the fort gets wind of the payroll being took like this.''

"Then he ought to rouse his men and get on the trail of those thieves,'' Ellen Garland said, coming over to stand beside Slocum. ''Mr. Slocum fought like ten men. I would be dead were it not for him!''

The marshal snorted and shook his head. The tips of his mustaches wobbled in tiny circles as he ground his teeth.

"Don't read it that way. He might have been in cahoots with them.''

"I didn't do this to myself to make it look like I'm innocent,'' Slocum said, lifting his left arm slightly. ''Dr. Woodson can tell you how badly hurt I was.''

The marshal turned and spat over the railing, not caring if anyone walked below. He hitched up his gun belt, glared at Slocum, and then said, "You get on over to the stage depot and report to McGrath. I want to run you in for being an accomplice on this here robbery. We been having a danged sight too many lately."

"He is innocent, sir," Ellen said, outraged. "And *you* go tell Mr. McGrath whatever you please. Mr. Slocum is too hurt to go gallivanting about on a fool's errand."

"Fool's errand, eh?" The marshal spat again, gave Slocum a hard stare, then trotted back down the wooden steps on his slightly bowed legs.

"What a disagreeable man," Ellen said, staring after the marshal. "How he could believe you had anything to do with the robbery is beyond me."

Slocum knew how that could happen. He hadn't been on the wrong side of the law in a long time, maybe a year or more, but wanted posters still circulated—and Slocum had a hard look about him. Coupled with the need to find a guilty party, the marshal didn't have to look farther than the doctor's office. Catching the outlaws responsible for the murders, horse thefts, and gold robbery was out of the question. Even if the cavalry rode out in company strength, the desperadoes were probably miles away by now.

"You find a place to stay?" Slocum asked.

"Why, yes, I have. The hotel down the street has several vacant rooms. The Sam Houston. I . . . I took the liberty of renting one, though I had no money. The clerk trusted me."

"How much are the rooms?"

"Fifty cents a night," Ellen said, staring at him with her combination of boldness and innocence. She lowered her voice and asked, "There's no need for each of us to take a room, is there? The bed's plenty big enough for us. The *two* of us."

Slocum fumbled in his shirt pocket and pulled out a

greenback. He handed it to her. "This will cover two nights' lodging." His hand pressed against the shirt pocket. Two dollars remained. Pain began creeping back into his broken arm, and he felt a need for a shot or two of whiskey to deaden it. The doctor's bottle was empty, but from the boisterous laughter and loud cries coming from down the street, Slocum knew Fort Griffin wasn't without its share of saloons.

"All right, John," she said, taking the money. "What are you going to do?"

"I ought to report to McGrath," he said, this being far from his real intention. "You go on over to the hotel. What room?"

"Two oh one," she said, reaching into a pocket and pulling out a large key. "At the head of the stairs. I have only the one key."

"You take it. I'll knock when I get over there. I won't be too long."

"It has been a hectic few days, hasn't it? And you need your rest." Ellen looked down at the floor, then cast a sidelong gaze at him as she smiled almost shyly. "If there's not something you'd rather do before going to sleep."

"Run on along," Slocum said, wondering why he was being so foolish and not going with her right away to the hotel. The pain was only a part of it, he knew. He couldn't count on getting paid by McGrath, and with only two dollars to his name, Slocum didn't have much in the way of fortune to take care of Ellen. She had lost everything in the stagecoach robbery, and he felt more than a passing responsibility for her.

Slocum followed her down the stairs, watched her head toward a rickety hotel with a poorly painted sign swinging out front proclaiming it to be the Sam Houston Hotel, then went the other way. The smell of stale beer and the sound of men trying to relieve the boredom of their lives drew Slocum. He looked into several saloons before finding a gambling hall to his liking.

He went inside and leaned against the bar. The barkeep came over, a wide smile on his lips almost hidden by his bushy mustache.

"Reckon I know your poison, mister. You're a whiskey drinkin' fellow, aren't you?"

"A shot of your strongest," Slocum said. "Need it to kill the pain."

"Hey, you're the shotgun messenger off the stagecoach, aren't you? Doc Woodson was in earlier tellin' everyone how he fixed you up. Boastin' and braggin' to beat the band, the doc was. Said he'd give a discount to anybody comin' in with wounds worse 'n yours."

"Glad to know I'm setting a standard for Fort Griffin," Slocum said. He knocked back the whiskey and almost choked. The doctor's bottle was smooth. This had the kick of a mule that had eaten loco weed. "Another," Slocum said, deciding he could afford another two bits for the whiskey. It was pricey, but he needed it.

"Make you a deal on the whole bottle," the barkeep offered.

"Rather find a game," Slocum said, looking longingly at the emptied shot glass. He had a dollar and a half left. Hardly enough for a good poker game, but he could find something else. Then he had to laugh. He wasn't ready for any poker game, not with a busted wing. "Faro," he said, knowing he wouldn't have to handle cards. "You got a spread somewhere?"

"Faro's not your kind of game, mister. I kin tell you're a risk taker. You want to get into a high stakes game."

"Reckon one of the other saloons might have a faro table running." Slocum moved to go. The barkeep reached out and stopped him.

"Wait, wait. The Lost Dutchman Dance Hall and Gambling Casino caters to everybody's tastes. We got the best durned faro dealer in the whole wide state of Texas. Upstairs.''

"Thanks,'' Slocum said, knowing there had to be more action going on in the Lost Dutchman than he saw downstairs. Two bored dance girls sat on the far side of the room, talking between themselves. The piano player idly picked at the keys, the tune vaguely familiar. Broad stairs at the left of the big room curved up and away to the second floor. Slocum went up slowly, each step taxing him a bit more. Seldom had he been so glad to reach the head of a staircase and see a dozen empty chairs beckoning to him. He went to the nearest one and slumped down.

Slocum straightened a mite when he saw the faro dealer. She was about his age and not what he would call pretty. Handsome fit her well. She had a dignity about her that immediately appealed to Slocum, as if she had seen the worst life had to offer and accepted it without complaint.

"A new player," she announced to the others sitting in front of the layout table. The dealer pushed back dull blond hair from her face and then got to shuffling the deck. Slocum watched her fingers fly and knew she was no novice. If she tried cheating by stacking pairs, he could not tell. He looked up into her green eyes, not the color of his but that of the Gulf of Mexico on a calm day.

"There's the soda card, gents,'' she said peeling off the top card and placing it faceup on top of the box. The remainder of the deck went into the faro box. "Place your bets.''

Slocum started with two–bit bets, winning slowly as he watched the game. He decided the dealer wasn't cheating, either through manipulation or a gaffed box. She didn't have to. The others at the table were so drunk they had no idea what they were doing. Given a fair game, the bank usually won only on splits and pairs.

The other three at the table might as well have forked over their money because of the way they bet.

Two more men joined the game, placing their bets on the table layout. The first card out on the turn was a loser, the second a winner for the players. One man immediately objected when the dealer went to rake in the double eagle he had placed on the loser.

"Didn't mean to bet that much. Meant to put a nickel there, not a gold piece." He grabbed the woman's wrist and squeezed down hard. Slocum saw pain flash across the woman's face. As quickly, she ground her teeth hard to keep from crying out. She wasn't going to show any weakness in the face of such blatant cheating.

"You bet, you lost. That belongs to the bank," she said between her clenched teeth.

"Well, missy, you got it wrong. I'm makin' a new bet," the man said. "I bet me and you can take that double eagle and buy ourselves a whole lot more fun."

"You lost. Let go of my wrist." Her green eyes turned from calm to blazing.

"This is a fair game, and you bet the gold piece," Slocum said, aware that he had an empty Colt Navy hanging at his hip. "If you can't afford to lose, you shouldn't bet."

"Butt out, cowboy. This is none of your concern." The other man turned and started reaching for his six–shooter. Slocum never hesitated. He half–stood and smashed his forehead into the man's nose. The man yelped and fell back. Slocum wasted no time following. His arm hurt like hell and he couldn't make a good fight of it. He kicked out and got his foot tangled in the other man's legs. Tumbling backward, arms and legs going in all directions, the man crashed into a wall and slid down slowly, stunned. He wasn't going to bother Slocum or the faro dealer any time soon.

The gambler who had seized the dealer's wrist swung around when he saw what had happened to his crony.

Slocum took a clumsy swing and connected with about as much force as a fly landing on a horse's rump. The gambler took a half step away from Slocum, not greatly bothered by the feeble punch.

"You got fire in your belly for a gimp," the man said. "You're gonna have to learn not to annoy your betters." He wound up and unloaded a haymaker that caught Slocum square in the jaw. Slocum reeled back and fell to the floor.

"Go get the marshal," the faro dealer told him. "Do it right now."

Slocum felt like a coward as he rolled onto the steps leading to the saloon below, but the woman was right. He couldn't handle these two by himself, not busted up the way he was and with an empty six-gun in his cross-draw holster. Before he reached the bottom step, he heard shots ring out behind him in the gambling hall.

"Somebody fetch the marshal!" Slocum bellowed. The barkeep glanced up, frightened, then rushed from behind the long wood bar and darted into the street. Slocum knew there wasn't much he could do upstairs, but he had to try. It might be too late if he waited for the marshal. The steps up were even harder to climb than before, because he knew he would find only death above.

5

Slocum heard the Lost Dutchman Dance Hall's swinging doors crash against the walls and knew the marshal was close. That didn't stop Slocum from taking the steps back into the casino two at a time. He reached behind him and found the thick–bladed knife in its sheath at the small of his back. It wasn't much against a man firing away with a six–shooter, but it was better than trying to fight with a broken arm.

Slocum stopped at the head of the stairs and stood with his mouth agape. People had died, but they weren't the ones Slocum would have thought. Standing behind the faro table, looking only a little flustered at the furor, stood the blond woman dealer. In her firm hand, she held a two–shot derringer. The white smoke drifting from the twin barrels told part of the story.

The rest of the tale lay spread out on the floor. Both men, the one Slocum had knocked down and the one who had decked him, had met their match in the lady gambler.

"They threw down on me," she said simply as she tucked the derringer back into the folds of her flaring skirt.

"I seen it, I did!" piped up one of the drunks at the table. The haze of whiskey had been burned away, and he sat bolt upright, eyes wide, and his double chins quivering slightly. "They tried to gun her down and Lottie here beat them to the draw."

"What's going on?" The marshal pushed past Slocum and stood, hand resting on the butt of his six-shooter. "Oh, my God," he muttered. "Not two more dead ones." The lawman dropped to his knees and pressed a hand against one man's chest.

"The other varmint's dead, too, Marshal Ryder. I seen it all. Lottie shot in self-defense. They thought to steal back what they'd lost, and she cut 'em down where they stood when they drew on her."

Slocum said nothing, wondering what thoughts rattled through the marshal's head. Fort Griffin probably had more than its share of killings, and two in one night strained the marshal's patience. Added to the disturbance caused by the stage robbery, it might be more than the marshal cared to deal with.

"I'll get them out of here," Ryder said. He went to the faro table and said, "Miss Dennison, this is most unusual. You have a witness that it was in self-defense."

"It was, marshal." The simple way she spoke told any caring to listen she had acted only to defend herself.

"I'm inclined to believe you. These two have been askin' for trouble ever since they blowed into town last week. You're an honorable woman, even if you deal faro."

"Ask the reverend about it, marshal," interrupted the witness. "Lottie's about the only one in Fort Griffin what goes to church every Sunday, 'ceptin' the reverend, of course. She's a God–fearin' woman.''

"I'm sure she is. That's not the question." Ryder looked from Lottie Dennison to the dead men and back. He nodded once, brisk and all business. "That's the way it is. Self–defense, pure and simple." As if Ryder saw him for the first time, the marshal's gaze coldly fastened on Slocum.

A finger stabbed out in Slocum's direction.

"You, Slocum. Get on downstairs. I was outside talkin' with McGrath, and he's got a wild hair up his ass about the stage robbery."

"Don't look so good for you, does it Marshal Ryder? Losing a stagecoach, a payroll, four men killed by high-waymen, now two more dead in a saloon. You're having a busy day," said the barkeep, standing just behind Slo-cum.

"You shut your tater trap, Tom," Ryder snapped. He stormed out, furious. Slocum was glad the lawman had left. Lead might have started flying if the man had stayed around a second longer. The marshal had been pushed to the edge and seemed inclined to go beyond it. He was a man too small for a big job.

"Don't worry about him. McGrath is fit to be tied, though," the barkeep said. Tom went to the dealer and looked over the spread. The coins from the last turn had not been touched on the table. The barkeep shoved them all in the woman's direction, saying, "Bank's the winner on this round."

Spinning, the barkeep shouted to the others in the room, "Gents, come on down and I'll stand the house for a drink. Free drinks!"

This produced a roar of approval. Slocum remained behind, going to the faro table.

"You handled yourself well," he said to the lady gambler. "I'm John Slocum." He thrust out his hand. For a moment, the woman stared at it, then smiled broadly and shook his hand, her grip as firm as any man's.

"I'm Carlotta Dennison," she said. "Why don't you go on down, have a free drink on Tom, since he doesn't do this too often, then come on back. I feel like I owe you."

"You did all the dirty work," Slocum said, tilting his head in the direction of the bodies on the floor. He studied the woman carefully for any sign of shock setting in after gunning down two men intent on ventilating her. She was pale but composed. Carlotta Dennison had an iron core under that good–looking exterior.

"You knock back that shot of whiskey. I reckon it's owed you—and come on up and play a few turns of faro at my table." The way she said it told Slocum his luck had changed.

He nodded and went downstairs, trying to keep his rubbery legs from wobbling. He had gone too far too fast in the past couple days and needed rest. Going to the bar, he accepted another shot of the fierce, potent rotgut. The tides of fire washed through him, starting from the pool in his belly and working out the pain he experienced in his arm. Slocum felt almost human when he put the shot glass on the bar. Almost.

And his mood shifted swiftly when the Abilene Stagecoach Company manager bustled over to him.

"There you are, Slocum. I mighta knowed you'd be swilling Tom's tarantula juice. You're nothing but a—" McGrath bit off the rest of the diatribe when he saw the way Slocum glared at him. Slocum had been pushed too much and wasn't going to take any guff off anyone, the stagecoach manager least of all.

"I told Marshal Ryder everything I know. Those owlhoots shot up the coach, killed Doc Bond, two passengers, and the station master. They stole the gold and the spare teams at the depot. They'd've drilled me and Ellen Garland, too, but we got away."

"The woman passenger? What became of her?"

"She's over at the Sam Houston Hotel," Slocum said. "She got me to Dr. Woodson and then went over there. I'd say you owe her plenty. She lost everything she had in that robbery."

"Don't go tellin' me what to do, Slocum. You're responsible. You should have stopped them."

"A company of cavalry would have had their hands full with those robbers," Slocum said. "They were tough hombres." Slocum felt drained and in no mood to continue the conversation. He had done all he could to protect the Abilene Stagecoach shipment and passengers. It galled him that he had failed.

"Don't expect to get any pay for this trip, Slocum. I swear, I will not pay you a plugged nickel!"

"You'll pay—in hell," Slocum said, turning his back to the manager. McGrath sputtered and stormed off. Slocum didn't much care what the man thought or did. It was all pretty much the same to him and didn't change what had happened.

Slocum fingered the few greenbacks he had won at the faro game and remembered what Carlotta Dennison had said about returning. Slocum was tempted to go straight to the hotel and Ellen Garland. She had promised him more than a place to sleep, and any woman that pretty was a powerful persuader. Yet he felt guilty about her. In spite of what he had told McGrath, Slocum worried that he might have done something differently that would have saved the passengers and Ellen's belongings.

"Don't whip yourself over nothing," the barkeep said, coming over. He poured another shot. "No, don't pay. The rest of these worthless slugs bellied up to my bar can pay from here on, but you get another one on the house. Ain't often a man will help out like you did. It's appreciated."

"Thanks, Tom," said Slocum, accepting the drink. It

was likely the only charity he was going to get in Fort Griffin, considering how the marshal and the stagecoach company manager acted. "Mind if I go back up and try my luck again? The first game was interrupted."

The barkeep shrugged and made a gesture indicating it was fine with him if Slocum went upstairs and lost enough to pay for all the free drinks given out by the management of the Lost Dutchman Dance Hall. Slocum drank the second shot of whiskey more slowly, savoring its burning all the way down his gullet. He wanted to lick the last drops off the rim of the glass but held back.

Slocum climbed the stairs again, strength returning to him. He settled onto the hard stool in front of Lottie Dennison and pulled out his money.

"You asked me to come back," he said. "I'm hoping you are right about Lady Luck riding on my shoulder."

"She's around. You have to hunt for her sometimes," Lottie said. The blond dealer shuffled expertly. Slocum watched her movements like a hawk. As far as he could tell, she didn't try manipulating the deck. She slid off the soda card and dropped it on top of the box.

"Ready for the first turn?" she asked.

Slocum nodded, placing a small wager on the five. He won. No matter how he played, he won. Beginning to bet on combinations, he still won. After running through the deck and ending up with the hock card, Slocum counted his money and saw he had won almost a hundred dollars.

"See?" Lottie said. "Luck is all around. You have to recognize her."

"And know when she's getting ready to smile on someone else?" Slocum pulled his money back, aware that Lottie had somehow gaffed the box. She had cheated so he could win, and he didn't have any idea how it was done. He had to credit her with being about the best faro dealer he'd ever seen, and he had been in his share of gambling halls.

He started to push a five-dollar greenback toward her in way of thanks, but the set to her lips told Slocum this was neither wanted nor appreciated.

"Again, thank you. This is going to save a lot more than a down–on his–luck shotgun messenger," Slocum said. He had enough money to help Ellen Garland get her on her way, wherever that might be. For the first time, Slocum realized how little he knew of the lovely raven–haired woman waiting for him.

"What are your plans?" Lottie asked.

"Don't have many, not with a broken arm. Some of the money goes to Dr. Woodson for his fine work."

"The Woodworker he calls himself. He's a hoot," Lottie said. "A good doctor, but a mite strange. I think he might have got kicked in the head by a mule when he was up in Oregon logging country plying his trade." She tipped her head to one side, as if sizing up Slocum. Unexpectedly she asked, "You ever deal?"

"Poker's my game. I prefer seven card stud, though draw poker has its moments, too."

"We can use another faro dealer. Doesn't require much in the way of dexterity. All you have to do is pull the cards from the box and keep track of what's been played on the casekeeper." Lottie indicated the abacus-like arrangement of wood beads on a metal slide wire.

"You have to be honest," Slocum added.

"That's a help, but not really expected. That is why Tom has ringers come in and gamble now and then to see if his dealers are playing square."

"You're mighty good," Slocum said. "I'm not anywhere as good with the cards."

Carlotta Dennison laughed, and the sound was liquid silver tumbling over a waterfall. "If you were half as good, I wouldn't offer you a job. I figure with your arm like that, you'll have to deal honest or everyone will see it."

"I couldn't even change stacks on the payout," Slocum answered, indicating that he knew of more than one way of stealing from the customers and the house. Many faro dealers weren't good enough cheats to stack the deck or palm cards and relied on simply not paying out the right amounts to the gamblers. The easiest of these ways was to push forward a tall stack of chips, palm one chip and shortchange the payout.

"Think on it. The job'll still be here tomorrow after you've had a good night's sleep and a decent breakfast." Lottie turned and motioned to three cowboys staggering up the stairs, indicating she had a table open and waiting for them.

Slocum tucked his winnings into his shirt pocket and backed away, watching Lottie carefully. He revised his earlier estimate of her. She was more than handsome. She had a beauty to her that was unusual but hidden under what seemed to be a burden of woe. Whatever her troubles, she had given him a new lease on life when he needed it most. If she meant it about a job, Slocum knew he could make enough to keep body and soul together until his arm healed enough to find a better job.

Stepping into the cold night, Slocum shivered slightly. It was hard to believe he and Ellen had spent the prior night out alone on the prairie, walking in circles because he was too bunged up to know better. The thought of the woman set his boots moving toward the hotel. Slocum paused in the lobby, worrying that the night clerk might question him about coming in so late to visit a single lady customer.

The man had jacked his feet up onto the desk and covered his face with a newspaper. From underneath the printed pages came a deep, resonant snoring. The clerk wasn't likely to stop anybody, much less someone who knew where he was going.

Slocum climbed the steep steps and found room 201 at the top. He knocked softly, wondering if Ellen would be waiting up for him.

The door opened a crack. He saw her bright blue eyes widen in joy. She opened the door all the way and he found himself surrounded by a powerful hug. She kissed him hard and stepped away, pulling him with her.

"I didn't think you'd come, John. I—"

"You thought I'd leave you?" Slocum took off his battered hat and placed it on the dresser. The Stetson had been brand–new when he'd left Abilene. Now it was filthy and filled with holes. The garrison cap he had worn through the entire Battle of Gettysburg had been in better condition after the three–day fight.

"I didn't know. Everything is so upsetting," she said, sitting on the edge of the bed, her hands folded primly in her lap.

Slocum groaned slightly as he pulled off his gun belt and sat beside her. His arm hurt like the devil, but the sight of the lovely woman did wonders to quell the pain.

"I talked to the stagecoach manager. McGrath. He said he was powerful sorry for your inconvenience and offered you fifty dollars. I've got it here." Slocum fumbled in his shirt pocket and pulled out three greenbacks, two twenties and a ten he had won at the Lost Dutchman Dance Hall.

Money that Carlotta Dennison had virtually given him.

Somehow, Slocum felt he was doing the right thing passing along half his winnings to Ellen. She was the one who had been inconvenienced the most. Slocum was used to being battered and shot up. Somehow, the young lady from Austin appeared to be from a different social class, one higher on the ladder of success.

"Why, that's wonderful. You have done so much for me, John. How can I repay you?" She asked the question, but the light in her bright eyes told Slocum she knew the answer. Her fingers lingered as they worked on his shirt. He had trouble getting the shirt off around all the bandages, but with the woman's help, he suc-

ceeded. She was downright eager when she got to pulling off his boots and underwear. He lay back on the bed,
trying to ignore the pain in his arm. With a half dozen
shots of liquor in his belly, Slocum was surprised that
he didn't slosh.

"See anything you'd like as reward?" Ellen Garland
spun around in the small room, turning fine pirouettes.
Each turn produced another unbuttoned button or loos-
ened tie. Her skirt slid down around her fine legs. The
dark–haired woman stepped lithely away, kicking the
skirt out of the way. As she bent, Slocum was treated
to the sight of her round, firm buttocks.

"I see plenty I like," he said, reaching his hand out
and stroking flesh enclosed in frilly garments. Ellen wiggled and giggled and shoved back so he took a handful
of her buttocks.

She turned slowly, her hand on his to keep it from
moving. She widened her stance and brought his hand
between her thighs. Ellen closed her eyes and sighed in
contentment as Slocum's fingers pressed into her most
intimate flesh.

Rubbing back and forth produced a flow of moisture
from deep inside. The oily lubricant greased his fingers
and let them slide slickly over her legs and all around
her nether lips. Ellen began shuddering as if he tortured
her.

"Can't take any more like that, John," she said in a
husky voice. "I need more. Can't stand just your hand.
I want *this!*" She reached over and grabbed for him.

It was Slocum's turn to groan as her hand circled his
hardening length. Her fingers tightened and began moving up and down. He was going to tell her he wanted
more, too, but she was already lifting her leg over his
and swinging onto the bed. Facing away from him, she
lifted up and arranged her undergarments. She lowered
her hips and Slocum fell into paradise.

"So nice, John, just what I wanted. What I needed."

Ellen leaned forward over his feet and grabbed the brass rail at the end of the bed. Using this as a support, she began lifting and dropping her hips. Sensations ripped through Slocum's body and threatened to rob him of his self–control.

Looking down, he saw her naked back and the way her buttocks splayed out. Watching as she rose and dropped gave him a view of entering her he had seldom witnessed. The sight of him entering and leaving her hot interior made Slocum even harder.

His strength flowed away as passion took its toll. He lay back on the bed and let the woman do what she wanted. It was plenty enough for him. The friction along his length mounted and her ardent moans of joy rose to tell him everything was just fine.

"I can't do this much longer, John," she gasped out. "Inside me, all inside me, it's so hot, so wonderfully hot!"

Her hips began flying like a shuttlecock, up and down, faster and faster. She bent forward, leaning against the brass rail, then sat upright. Every movement took another fraction of Slocum's control. He was burning up inside, fiery white–hot tide rising along his length. When he blasted apart like a stick of dynamite, Ellen groaned and threw back her head.

Long hair flying, she bucked like a bronco and took every inch of him deep inside. She twisted and turned and Slocum thought he knew how a cow felt being milked. Her tightness surrounding him turned almost painful as her inner muscles closed on his buried length.

Then Ellen sagged forward, her hair tickling his legs. She turned around, her long leg slipping over his body. She edged up and lay alongside him, her fingers tangling in the thick hair of his chest. Slocum let the warmth suffuse his body and knew he could easily sleep, in spite of the pain in his shoulder and broken arm.

"I never thought it could be like this, John," she said.

"I haven't had much practice at this. Not even with Willie."

"You could have fooled me. It was fine, Ellen, just fine. When I get some rest, we'll—" Slocum was half asleep, so it took him longer than usual to pick up on what Ellen Garland had just said. He rolled away from her and lifted himself up. "Who's Willie?"

"Willie Prentice, my fiancé. He's why I came to Fort Griffin."

Slocum went cold inside. He was sleeping with another man's betrothed. The circumstances didn't matter. He just was. Pushing himself away even farther, he sat up and swung his legs over the edge of the bed. Dizziness hit him like a hammer blow to the head, but he paid it no mind.

"Why didn't you tell me about Prentice?"

"There was never any right time, John." Ellen didn't sound contrite as much as she did embarrassed. "You and I, well, circumstances were such that it seemed natural. With Willie, he's such a hothead."

"You said you were looking for him. That doesn't sound like he'd sent for you."

"He didn't. I'm worried about him. He came up here to get away from my parents. They don't like him one little bit. I . . . I'm afraid he may have fallen in with bad company. I want to marry him and we can go away somewhere."

Slocum heard more in Ellen Garland's story than she was putting into the words. He didn't press her for details. What worried him the most was the part about her boyfriend running with outlaws. The band that had held up the stage had been brutal and thorough. How many gangs would be in Texas working the Abilene–Fort Griffin stagecoach route?

Slocum doubted there would be more than one, and that meant Willie Prentice might have been in with the owlhoots responsible for the robbery. He didn't mention this to Ellen. She seemed distraught enough.

"I didn't mean to upset you, John."

"You reckon Willie Prentice's in The Flats?"

"Why, yes. That's why I came here. I got a letter from him saying he was coming this way."

"How long ago?" Slocum began dressing. He was a man of honor. He would never have slept with another man's betrothed if he had known. That way lay only blood feuds and a passel of trouble he wasn't willing to take on, even for a woman as lovely as Ellen.

"Almost a month. It took me a while to get this far, after I trailed him to Abilene. I had to—"

"I'll ask around." Slocum clumsily fastened his gun belt around his middle. It didn't ride right, but it didn't matter. There weren't any rounds in the Colt Navy.

"John, don't go. Stay." The pain in Ellen's voice almost made Slocum stop pulling on his boots. Almost. He felt betrayed and angry, more at himself than at the woman. He ought to have found out why she was coming to a dead-end town like Fort Griffin.

"I know where to find out if Prentice is around," Slocum said. He left Ellen sobbing in the room. His fury burned away any remorse he might have had about hurting her. She had been a willing bed partner, and she had gotten him there under false pretenses. He hadn't thought Ellen Garland was like that, but Slocum knew he hadn't been thinking straight.

The pain kept him on edge—and he knew an outraged fiancé would add to that pain, if Willie Prentice found out what had been happening between his promised and John Slocum.

Cold air cut Slocum's face as he stepped into the street. Behind, from the lobby of the hotel, came the loud snores of the clerk. Down the street the saloons roared on into night with frantic activity. Slocum rubbed the sleep from his eyes and walked toward one, not really caring if he found Willie Prentice. He had just wanted to get away from Ellen Garland and the revelation she had sprung on him.

"She's going to marry a man likely to have been responsible for holding up the stage," grumbled Slocum. He turned into the first saloon he came to. The bright light from gas lamps around the walls made him squint. He held up his hand to shield his eyes. When he could see better, Slocum went cold inside.

At the far end of the bar stood Jack Porbaugh. Slocum started to back out of the saloon when Porbaugh glanced up and spotted him.

"Slocum!" Porbaugh shouted, shoving aside the man next to him at the bar. He stepped out to get a clear field of fire. "You're a dead man, Slocum!"

Jack Porbaugh went for his six-shooter, and few in Texas were as quick or deadly.

6

The room around him moved as if dipped in molasses. He saw Jack Porbaugh going for his six–gun and responded. His own hand slid across his belly, flashing for the Colt in the cross–draw holster. Slocum didn't get halfway when he realized he would be dead. His six–shooter was empty. There hadn't been a chance to buy more ammunition.

If he kept standing where he was, he'd end up a corpse with an empty six–shooter in his hand.

Slocum blinked, and saw Porbaugh had his gun half out of his holster. The man's face had contorted into a mask of pure hate, and mingling with the hatred came a look of triumph. Porbaugh knew he had Slocum dead to rights.

Slocum didn't try to check his movement going for his six–gun. Instead, he spun to his left. His right arm was exposed to Porbaugh's deadly accurate fire, but his body was moving to the left when the first leaden slug ripped past him. Slocum felt fire blaze across his back. Porbaugh had nicked him but hadn't gotten in a killing shot. Slocum landed hard in the sawdust on the saloon floor, new pain jolting him. Scrambling fast, he kicked and got behind a table. Two more rounds blew away splinters above his head. He reached for the sheathed knife at his back, knowing it wasn't much of a weapon to use against a gunman as good as Jack Porbaugh.

"You're a damned coward, Slocum. Draw, damn your eyes. Get out here and *die!*" Porbaugh marched forward, ready to kill a man he had hated for more than a year.

Two more slugs tore through the beer–stained table where Slocum huddled. Chancing a quick look out, Slocum saw he had a faint chance to escape. Porbaugh must have just ridden into town. Like Slocum and many others who depended on their six–shooters, Porbaugh kept his hammer resting on an empty cylinder to keep the tricky percussion caps from going off accidentally while in the saddle.

Before Porbaugh could reload, Slocum got his feet under him, judged distances, and dived through a side window. Glass shattered and cut at his arms and back, adding new scratches to the others he had been accumulating since the stagecoach robbery. Slocum hit hard in the alley and rolled. His broken arm sent lances of pure agony into his body. He stumbled to his feet and tried to put as much distance between him and The Jackal as he could. He knew when it was better to retreat than to stand and foolishly fight.

"Slocum!" he heard Porbaugh scream at the top of his lungs. "Slocum!"

Getting to his feet, Slocum stumbled along the alley beside the saloon. He got turned around and lost his sense of direction for a moment. Behind the saloon Slocum stopped to get his bearings and catch his breath. He knew Porbaugh would be on his trail like a bloodhound. The two had ridden together a year and a half earlier, over in New Mexico Territory. They had always drifted away at the first trace of the law, stealing a steer or two to stay alive during hard times. Slocum had never been easy around Porbaugh because of his fiery temper and quick trigger. All the while they had ridden together, Jack Porbaugh had never killed anyone, but he had sent more than one man to the doctor with serious wounds.

But the law had caught Porbaugh and the man had been convicted of murder in Silver City. Word had reached Slocum that Porbaugh thought he was responsible for the arrest. Slocum hadn't even known of anything Porbaugh had done that would land him in jail, other than the cattle rustling, but more than one friend had warned Slocum that Porbaugh had sworn vengeance.

One thing Slocum knew all too well: Jack "The Jackal" Porbaugh never forgot a slight. He could turn into a wild-eyed killer, given the slightest provocation. It was only pure bad luck that Porbaugh had spotted Slocum the instant he had walked into the saloon. And what was Porbaugh even doing in Fort Griffin? This Texas town was out of the way, even if it did have something of a reputation for being a gambler's haven. Fort Worth, Jacksboro, San Antonio, Austin, all were better places for the gamblers riding the circuit.

"Slocum, you're a dead man. Come on out and let me put a bullet into your yellow belly. I want to see you die slow. You set me up and got me convicted. I don't forget. I don't!"

Slocum knew The Jackal was trying to spook him. If he flushed from cover now, Porbaugh's deadly six-shooter would cut him down. He had his heavy breathing under control, but did he dare risk staying in hiding?

The chance to flee turned to death if he stirred. Jack

Porbaugh stepped into the alley, gun in his thick–fingered hand. He widened his stance and waited for any hint of movement before opening fire.

"Slocum!"

Slocum pressed back into the wall, wanting to fade into it. He clutched his knife, deciding a quick toss would only leave him disarmed. Porbaugh had a better chance to kill him than Slocum did of sticking the Arkansas toothpick in The Jackal's chest.

Moving like the Grim Reaper, Porbaugh began walking down the alley. His head swayed back and forth, looking for any hint of movement. Slocum knew he was going to be a dead man in jig time. The white of his bandaged left arm would catch the light when Porbaugh took another step. Slocum tensed, ready to fling his knife. It might distract Porbaugh or cause his aim to be off just a tad.

What would happen then, Slocum knew all too well. Grappling with Porbaugh would be his end. With a broken arm and more cuts than he could count, Slocum was no match for a healthy, wrathful man.

"Jack, the marshal's coming," came the cry from the far end of the alley. "We got to go *now*."

"I ain't found Slocum yet," Porbaugh called over his shoulder. He turned back to the hunt. "You're here, Slocum. I can smell you. You're sweatin' blood, you're so scared."

"Jack!" There was no denying the urgency of the call from Porbaugh's crony.

Jack Porbaugh paused, just a step away from discovering Slocum's hiding place. He suddenly turned and stalked off. Slocum let out a lungful of air he hadn't even realized he was holding. Weakness washed across him, and he almost collapsed. He took a few deep breaths to calm his racing heart. He now knew how a rabbit felt when chased by a hungry coyote. It wasn't an emotion he wanted to share again.

Peering around the piles of crates he had taken refuge behind, Slocum saw only emptiness stretching to the outskirts of Fort Griffin. If he had an ounce of common sense, he would head for the city limits and keep on going, on foot if he had to, but better on horseback.

Jack Porbaugh would make sure he was pushing up prairie posies if Slocum stayed in Fort Griffin much longer. And the worst part of it was that Slocum didn't really know what had gone on back in Silver City. When he had heard Porbaugh was in jail, he had hightailed it. He might have tried to break The Jackal out, but that hadn't seemed prudent.

Slocum hadn't owed Jack Porbaugh anything. They had ridden together but had never been friends. And the wanted posters on his own head had weighed on Slocum then. Quite a spell had passed and the heat from those warrants had died down a mite—or so he hoped. Porbaugh showing up as he had in Fort Griffin made Slocum wonder if The Jackal hadn't taken up a new line of work.

Bounty hunting was dangerous work, but it paid well. And who better to hunt down a criminal than another?

Slocum reversed his path down the alley and carefully peered around the corner of the saloon. To his relief, Porbaugh had vanished. In the middle of the alley, hands on his hips, stood Marshal Ryder. The lawman was clearly agitated, shouting incoherently at someone still on the boardwalk and out of Slocum's view. The marshal threw his hands up and stormed off.

Slocum hoped the lawman was on Porbaugh's trail.

He started to return to the Sam Houston Hotel and Ellen, then stopped. Nothing had changed, and Slocum wasn't going to use the woman as a shield. He needed ammo for his six-shooter, but even then he would be at a disadvantage in any fight with the gunman. Slocum remembered Jack Porbaugh as a man living on the edge of life and death, always ready to draw and start firing.

"Willie Prentice," Slocum said softly to himself. With information about Ellen Garland's boyfriend, he could discharge any responsibility he felt toward her. The money had gone a ways, but getting her back together with Prentice would complete his obligation.

As he walked, Slocum began to lurch. His brush with the Jackal had taken more out of him than he had thought. The glass shards stung like a hornet's nest had been shoved down the back of his neck. Slocum walked past the saloon and saw the tight knot of men inside, arguing over the broken window. He kept moving, his legs turning weaker with every step.

Somehow, Slocum got to the steps leading up to Dr. Woodson's office. One step at a time, Slocum got to the office door and rapped sharply. He heard a mumbled response inside. By the time the sawbones had thrown on a robe and come to the door, Slocum fell through into the man's powerful arms.

"Ah, Slocum, you are back. I wondered how long it would be. You had the aspect of man intent on destroying himself."

"Got the money for fixing me up before." Slocum fumbled in his pocket and shoved a twenty in the doctor's direction.

"Good, good, usually my patients forget my fine works. Is this a deathbed gesture or does life still burn brightly within your frame?" The doctor clucked to himself as he lifted Slocum bodily and dropped him onto the examining table.

"Not so bad this time," Slocum got out. "A few scratches."

"Glass, from the debris left in the wounds," Woodson said, peering at Slocum's back. "You need a new shirt. Let me paint you up with disinfectant, and I'll see what's in my trunk. Patients tend to pay off in clothing, most of it too small for me."

Woodson hummed as he worked. Slocum winced a

few times, then fell into a numbness that served him well. The doctor finished his work and dropped a worn but clean shirt across Slocum's lap.

"That should fit you. I've got a good eye for such things, or so my wife tells me."

"Didn't mean to interrupt you. It's late."

"Not to worry. I don't live here. My wife's thrown me out of the house again," Woodson said. Slocum couldn't tell if the doctor enjoyed this prospect. "Is my curiosity to be served if I ask what happened to you?"

"I ran afoul of someone who doesn't think too kindly of me," Slocum said. "You ever hear of Jack Porbaugh?"

"The Jackal?" Woodson let out a low whistle. "Slocum, if he is after you, think on leaving The Flats. He comes and goes, never with the marshal's approval."

"Is there money on his head?"

"Might be," Woodson allowed. "You'd have to ask Marshal Ryder. All I know of Porbaugh is secondhand, but he's put more than one man into the potter's field south of town. I wish he would kill someone with a few dollars. My brother–in–law can use the money."

"He's the undertaker," Slocum said.

"Dangerous man, Porbaugh. Word is that he is involved with rustling. He and his band sniff around Fort Griffin outside of The Flats, looking to steal cavalry beeves."

Slocum heaved a sigh. He might have known Porbaugh wasn't engaged in anything legal. If Marshal Ryder got wind of Porbaugh's feud with him, Slocum knew the lawman would start leafing through old wanted posters. There was no telling what he might find.

"You hear rumors," Slocum said. "Hear any about a man named Willie Prentice?"

Woodson scratched his stubbled chin, thought hard, and then shook his head. "Name doesn't ring any bells. So many folks come and go through The Flats that it's getting hard to keep up with them. Used to be a peace-able enough place, 'cept Saturday nights when the troop-ers came to town. No more. Every night's a debauch.''

"How much more for fixing me this time?" Slocum jumped to the floor, steadied himself, and struggled to put on the shirt. Woodson helped him. The shirt was loose around Slocum, but it accommodated his broken arm better this way.

"You make life interesting, Slocum. Don't go getting yourself killed until you play your hand with Porbaugh. I want to know how that comes out."

"Thanks, Doc."

Slocum made his way to the door, then paused when Woodson cleared his throat.

"Slocum, you might try asking Tom over at the Lost Dutchman Dance Hall about this Prentice fellow. Tom's got his ear to the ground more 'n anybody else in town."

"How late's the saloon open?" Slocum studied the sky and saw that it was only an hour or so until dawn. It had been a hell of a night.

"Tom's there all the time. Owns the place. I reckon he'll turn it over to the day barkeep come six A.M. You got an hour to get over there."

"Thanks. I appreciate it."

"Send me some more paying customers," Dr. Wood-son said cheerfully, closing and locking the door behind Slocum.

Taking the steps down carefully, Slocum knew he was about at the end of his rope. He sat on the bottom step and considered what to do. Tom over at the Lost Dutch-man or back to the hotel and Ellen Garland.

"Tom, you better have what I need to know." Slocum wanted to help Ellen Garland find who she had come to Fort Griffin to locate, so he could move on. Until he knew where Willie Prentice was, he wouldn't feel right.

The walk from the doctor's office to the saloon dragged into a trek of a thousand miles. Slocum was

about ready to fall down when he pushed through the
Lost Dutchman's swinging doors. The crowd had
thinned to one drunk sleeping at a back table and another
leaning against the bar talking with Tom.

From the way they spoke, Slocum doubted the man
was a customer. It might be Tom's day barkeep. He
walked over and leaned heavily against the bar.

"Slocum, you're back sooner than I thought. Get you
a drink?"

"No, thanks. I just came by for some information."

"Wait a minute. Hey, Curly, this here's the gent who
stood up for Lottie earlier in the night. I'm tryin' to get
him to come to work as a faro dealer."

Slocum's eyes widened. Carlotta Dennison had mentioned it to him, and Slocum had thought the woman ran
the gambling upstairs. Tom might take a cut, but the
way the lady faro dealer had talked, the concession was
all hers.

"We're partners, Lottie and me," Tom said. "The
day she came into town, I knew she was going to make
me a mint. I let her use the tables and we split the take.
She's got final say–so on hiring and firing, but I know
a good prospect when I see one. I've been in the dance
hall business for well nigh eight years now."

"And she already mentioned her offer?" Slocum
heaved a sigh. He felt himself getting tangled in a web.
Small towns were like this, but he wanted nothing more
than to be on his way.

"She did. It was plain as day on her face when she
closed the tables a few hours back."

"So, are you going to work for her?" asked Curly.
The man ran his hand through hair so straight it might
have been ironed flat. "It gets lonely around this place.
If you covered for her now and again, maybe she'd come
on downstairs for a drink."

Slocum saw that Curly hoped to improve his prospects
with Lottie if someone relieved her at dealing faro. From

the way Tom talked, he might have designs on her, too.

"I might be interested. Can't say right now."

"You looked plumb tuckered out," Tom said. "Get some sleep and make your decision."

"I will do that," Slocum said. His fatigue–numbed brain nudged him back to why he had come to the Lost Dutchman. He shifted weight on his feet and leaned more against the bar. "I just wanted to ask after a cuss who might be hanging around Fort Griffin. His name's Willie Prentice. Either of you heard of him?" Slocum saw recognition flash on both men's faces. They exchanged quick glances Slocum found indecipherable.

Tom cleared his throat and said, "Slocum, why don't you come on back around sundown."

"Sundown?" Slocum saw from the light slanting through the saloon windows that it was hardly sunrise. "Why then?"

"You might get an answer to where Prentice is," Tom said, licking his lips and increasingly uneasy at the prospect that Slocum wanted to find Willie Prentice.

"Who knows him? You?"

"No, not me or Curly." Tom cleared his throat again and avoided Slocum's eyes. "Ask Lottie. She knows."

7

"John, you came back." Ellen Garland tried to hold back tears. "I didn't mean for you to go like that. I—"

"I've been hunting for Willie Prentice. There's a chance I can find out where he is, but it'll have to wait until sundown."

"Oh," Ellen said, chewing on her lower lip. She brushed away tears. "It must have come as quite a shock to you, that I'm engaged to be married to Willie."

Slocum didn't want to talk about it. He knew he should have found another room, maybe in another hotel, but he was too beaten to make the effort. He felt rode hard and put away wet. Sitting on the edge of the bed, he groaned as pain rippled through his body. The cuts and scrapes Dr. Woodson had dabbed with tincture of iodine burned as if liquid fire had been smeared over his body.

"That's not the shirt you were wearing earlier." Ellen peeled Slocum's shirt back and gasped. "What happened?"

"It's hard tracking down Prentice," Slocum said. He lay back, clinging to the side of the bed. He felt guilty moving over any closer to Ellen Garland. She wasn't what he had thought. The woman belonged to another man, and he had trespassed.

"John?" Ellen's hand rested lightly on his shoulder. He mumbled. The words didn't form quite right, and it hardly mattered. "John?" That was all he heard. He slept heavily, his body demanding rest before going on anymore.

Stirring, Slocum sneezed and came awake completely, his hand reaching for his Colt Navy. He felt only the bandages on his left arm. Still more asleep than awake, he panicked and sat up. New pain shot through him, but it wasn't as bad as it had been when he'd drifted off to sleep. Or was passing out closer? He couldn't remember too well.

"I thought you would sleep around the clock," Ellen said, sitting in the straight-backed chair near the room's single window. "I bought some food for us, and got a few things using the money you gave me."

"Money?" Then Slocum remembered how he had given Ellen Garland half his winnings and told her it came from the Abilene Stagecoach Company. "I need to buy some things, too."

"I took the liberty of buying ammunition for you. I didn't know how much to get. Is this enough?"

"Enough," he said, seeing what she had purchased. This act of generosity startled him. Then he realized she might not feel the way he did. He had a strict code of honor about sleeping with another man's betrothed. That was as bad as if he had committed adultery. Of all the lessons he had learned from his father and mother, respect for women and the sanctity of marriage were foremost.

Slocum clumsily loaded the Colt Navy and put it into his holster. It felt better there, and he felt better knowing it was ready for action.

"Did you really find someone who knows where Willie is?" Ellen's anxious attitude told him where her real affections lay. "You weren't just putting me on?"

"I was told who might know where he is. The source is reliable," Slocum said, thinking of the lady gambler. Carlotta Dennison had shown gratitude and even honesty, paying her bills. He wasn't sure if the money he had won at faro came from Tom's pocket or Lottie's—and didn't much care. The service he had rendered helped both the owner of the Lost Dutchman and the faro dealer.

"You've done so much for me, John. I hardly know how to—"

"Let me have some of those victuals," he said, derailing her gratitude. It had put him in a bad situation. Slocum didn't want to deal any more with it, if he could avoid it. When he found Willie Prentice for her, Slocum would take another room. He might even do it before he located her boyfriend.

"Here," she said, passing over a paper–wrapped package. He found some smoked meat inside. With a large hunk of bread from a loaf, he wolfed down the simple meal. It couldn't have been better if she had given him a rare Delmonico steak smothered in onions. All Slocum missed was a cup of hot coffee to wash it all down.

As he ate, Ellen spoke, almost to herself, but loud enough for him to understand her words. "I must have known Willie forever, at least most of my life. We grew up together in Austin, but my folks never liked him. Too wild and unpredictable, they said. There was always something about him that drew me."

Slocum licked up the last of the bread crumbs, wishing there were more. He tried not to get sucked into the story Ellen was telling. It was too familiar.

"He left to find his fame and fortune. Why he came to Fort Griffin, I don't know. This place has a reputation. Gambling. Doc Holliday is a sometime resident here. The Flats, they call this place."

"Did your people run you off or did you run away?" Slocum asked.

"A little of both," Ellen admitted. "Life became impossible, especially with my papa. He never stopped telling me how lazy Willie was and how he would come to no good. There was a little trouble, but it wasn't Willie's fault."

Slocum regretted having said anything at all. The story always sounded the same. Ellen Garland came from a good family wanting her to better herself by marrying up in society. She had fallen for a wastrel, a criminal in the making, and that had set the sparks flying.

"About sundown," Slocum said, peering out the window past Ellen. "It's time for me to ask my questions."

"Let me come with you. I can—"

"Where I'm going, you wouldn't be comfortable," Slocum said.

"I don't care!" Ellen's cheeks showed bright rosy spots of passion.

"You won't be allowed in, where I have to go," he amended. He saw this hit her hard. She thought he meant he would be asking the soiled doves about her betrothed. Slocum didn't care what went through Ellen's mind, as long as she let him be.

"John, you don't have to do this for me."

"I feel obligated, after all that's . . . happened," he finished lamely. He stood and settled his cross–draw holster at his hip. He reached over and gripped the ebony handle a few times to be sure his broken left arm didn't get in his way. More limber and freer from pain than before, Slocum knew he was ready for anything that happened.

He left without another word. He went downstairs and into the street, aware of the room clerk's surprised stare as he passed through the lobby. Slocum turned down the dusty main street and walked into the long shadow he cast. Sleeping the entire day had done him a world of good.

Pausing before he entered the Lost Dutchman Dance Hall, Slocum considered what he would say to Lottie. He needed a job, and she had offered a good one to him, one he could ably handle with a broken arm. But would he muddy the waters asking after Willie Prentice? The only way he could tell was to make the effort.

Slocum went in and waved to Tom and Curly behind the bar. Tom motioned for him to come over.

"Good seeing you, Slocum. You gonna take the job Lottie offered?"

"I need to speak with her, but I'm leaning in that direction," Slocum said. "Is she already at the faro table?"

"She's got quite a crowd now. Several cowboys blowed in here and went straight up to lose their money." Tom laughed. "Lottie's the best thing that's happened to this saloon in years."

"She hasn't been here too long?" asked Slocum.

"Only a few weeks, but she surely does brighten the old Lost Dutchman. Lovely woman."

Tom leaned over the bar, as if telling Slocum something in strict confidence. His voice was pitched loud enough for Curly to overhear. "Curly's been trying to make time with Lottie ever since I hired her. She won't have a thing to do with him, though."

"Tom," Curly said, blushing. The barkeep turned away.

"She's savin' herself for me," Tom went on. Slocum wasn't sure if Tom was joking or seriously thought that he had a chance with the blond gambling lady.

"I'll sit in on the game for a turn or two," Slocum said. "When she gets a break, I'll talk to her."

Slocum went up the steps and froze when he reached the top. Five men sat at Lottie's faro spread. His hand flashed to the butt of his six–shooter, but he didn't draw. He backed down the stairs, keeping a sharp eye on Jack Porbaugh's broad back. The Jackal's loud voice ought to have warned him, but Slocum had been lost in his own worries.

He got back to the saloon's main floor without Porbaugh seeing him. Slocum heaved a sigh of relief and started out the front doors when Marshal Ryder pushed in.

"Slocum, I want a word with you. What do you know about Jack Porbaugh?"

"Why do you ask, marshal?" Slocum fought to keep from looking guiltily over his shoulder to see if Porbaugh overheard. The hairs on the back of his neck twitched.

"Heard rumors that you and him rode together over in New Mexico."

"I've ridden with quite a few men in my day. That's what happens when you're a drifter." Slocum wanted to give the impression he was only passing through Fort Griffin and not worthy of the marshal's concern.

"He's a damned rustler. I can't prove it, but I feel it in my bones. I've seen enough outlaws in my day to know he's a bad one." Ryder's whip–thin body jerked from side to side nervously, his skeletal hand stroking over the butt of his holstered six–gun. Slocum had seen men like this before. They usually got gunned down for their high–strung ways. A gunman like the Jackal would see the marshal touching his hogleg once too often and think he was being drawn down on. Blood always flowed when Jack Porbaugh's six–shooter cleared leather.

To get the marshal onto a different track, Slocum almost asked after Willie Prentice. Something warned him not to let that name slip free of his lips. He clamped his teeth shut tightly and waited. The marshal eyed him hard, then spun and walked away, spurs clanking. From behind, on the stairs, Slocum heard heavy footfalls. He didn't have time to go after the marshal and avoid Porbaugh and his gang. Instead, Slocum sank into a chair, his back to the room.

He hunched his shoulders and bent forward to hide his injured arm. He didn't know if Porbaugh had taken notice of it the night before. The Jackal had been intent on plugging him. Maybe Porbaugh hadn't seen his injuries.

"She's as purty as a royal flush," one of Porbaugh's men avowed.

"You keep your hands off her, Hank, or I'll hogtie you and drag you behind my horse from here to El Paso."

"Ah, Jack, it ain't like that."

"Better not let me catch you sniffin' around her," The Jackal warned. The rest of his men fell silent as the gang left the Lost Dutchman. Slocum bent over and watched from the corner of his eye until the doors stopped swinging. Only then did he straighten and heave a sigh of relief. He had six rounds in his Colt Navy. That would have taken one shot for each of Porbaugh's men—and nothing for The Jackal.

Slocum saw how Tom stared at him but said nothing. Slocum climbed the stairs and saw Lottie standing at her table, alone and looking forlorn. He sank onto the end stool.

"You came by to take the job?"

"I just might," Slocum said, "but it doesn't look as if you need two dealers."

"There are other games. We've got a keno rig in the

back room Tom's never set up. That would bring 'em flocking in.''

Carlotta Dennison tried to put up a brave front, but Slocum saw how disturbed she was after speaking with Jack Porbaugh. He wanted to find out what the flap was, but he owed Ellen information on her boyfriend. Coughing to clear his throat, he tried to put the words in the right order.

"Go on, Slocum, spit out what you want to ask. I'm a big girl. I can take just about anything you want to say." Lottie's challenge gave him the impetus needed to get the words flowing.

"I'm looking for someone," Slocum said. "Willie Prentice. Heard tell you might know of him."

Whatever Slocum had expected, Lottie's reaction wasn't it. Her mouth opened, closed, then she burst out crying. Lottie turned from him and dashed off, going to a door at the rear of the room.

"Wait, Lottie, I didn't mean to upset you." Slocum was slow getting off the stool. By the time he got around the table and reached the back door, Lottie had already run down the back stairs and was fleeing down the alley.

Slocum wondered if he ought to tell Tom about this, then decided he had caused Lottie's distress, so it was up to him to soothe her ruffled feathers, if he could figure out what the problem was. Fort Griffin was filled with riddles. It was about time he solved a few of them.

Taking the steps two at a time, he raced down and pounded along the alley, hunting for Lottie. Slocum skidded to a halt and stared down a narrow gap between the saloon and the store next door. Empty. He hurried along the alley, looking left and right. Wherever Carlotta Dennison had run, she had lost him in the wink of an eye. Going to the larger street, Slocum searched for her.

Lottie had vanished into thin air.

"You needin' something, mister?" came a whiskey-rough voice from behind him. Slocum saw the owner of the general store sweeping dust from the boardwalk in front of his door.

"You might be able to help," Slocum said, walking up the three steps. He perched on the railing and watched as the old man went about his work. "Not needing anything from your stock, but some information would go a long way."

"Talk's cheap," the man said, not even looking up as he kept sweeping.

"Lottie Dennison, the lady who deals faro at the Lost Dutchman. What can you tell me about her?"

"Not much. She's a nice, God–fearing woman. Don't often see her like working in a dive like the Lost Dutchman Dance Hall."

"How's that?"

"Goes to church every Sunday, is honest as the day is long, never whores around like them women usually do."

"She have a regular boyfriend?"

"Nope."

Slocum knew the store owner was turning chary with his gossip. "Where does she live?"

"Can't rightly say. Don't even know anyone who might. She keeps to herself. Some folks are like that." The man rested on his broom handle and cast a gimlet eye at Slocum, clearly conveying that Slocum might keep more to himself and ask fewer questions.

"Much obliged," Slocum said, dropping from the railing and walking along the boards.

Slocum went into a few other saloons, carefully asking after Lottie Dennison. Most of the men were in awe of the lovely gambler, telling of going to the Lost Dutchman for little more than losing a few dollars at Lottie's faro game. He heard tales of how she had taken up with Doc Holliday and was on the run from the cold–eyed gambler. Another tale spoke of her being from a rich family back East, come West to find adventure. Still another story that seemed more popular about her mysterious origins convinced Slocum no one knew the first detail of Carlotta Dennison's life. This story went that she sought a husband, and wouldn't budge from Fort Griffin until she found one.

But no one knew where she lived or how she spent her time when not dealing turns at faro. Slocum considered finding the Fort Griffin preacher and asking him about Lottie, but he held that back as a last resort. He knew he had upset her greatly, but Lottie would return to her tables eventually. When she did, Slocum would find out what spooked her like a hen chased by a fox.

8

"Have you seen Lottie?" Slocum asked Tom. The barkeep frowned and shook his head.

"Don't know what happened to her. This isn't like her, not at all. Lottie's the most reliable dealer I ever hired." Tom looked around, as if she might turn up any minute. When he didn't see her, he toyed with his waxed mustaches and said to Slocum, "That job's yours right now. We got a gaggle of buffalo hunters comin' in from the range. When those boys get down to serious drinkin', they want to gamble, and when they gamble, they ain't got the sense God gave a goose."

Slocum knew the skinners well. He had hunted with a band of them for almost four months. The work had been dirty, smelly, and backbreaking. He had been a sniper for the Confederacy and knew his way around rifles. Setting up a tripod for a heavy Sharps and shooting every wooly buffalo that came into his open sights hadn't been any fun, but it had been profitable. Slocum wouldn't want to go back with the skinners, but he knew they were the kind of men who spent half their life on the prairie, and he liked them.

"I reckon I can do about everything but shuffle. If you have somebody who could do that at the end of every turn, I can get Lottie's table up and bringing in chips before you know it. Or she mentioned you have a goose in the back room. I can start a keno game. The shinners always liked that one."

"They understand it better than poker," Tom agreed. "I can't spare anyone to run up every time you need shufflin' done, Slocum. The keno rig is a good idea. When did she tell you about the rig?"

Slocum didn't want to explain that he had been responsible for running off Carlotta Dennison. He just shrugged and let that be his answer. The cowboys and skinners coming into the Lost Dutchman Dance Hall kept Tom from asking any more questions Slocum didn't cotton much to answering.

"Curly, you get the keno rig set up for Slocum. Then you get on back here at the bar. This is gonna be one helluva night."

Curly dragged the goose, a large rotating clay pot containing numbered ivory balls, from the storeroom and helped Slocum get it upstairs. Slocum spent only a few minutes getting the keno table set up and began his spiel. He had played the game often enough to know what the keno dealers said to entice patrons. When he began turning the crank and getting the numbered balls out, he found himself facing a sea of unshaven, smelly buffalo hunters.

The game ran smoothly and enough of the skinners won that Slocum had no trouble getting more to play. And the more that played, the greater the house's take. By the time a few cavalry troopers drifted in to try their luck, the Lost Dutchman was packed to overflowing.

Now and then Slocum glanced over in the direction of Lottie's faro spread. She hadn't returned. He wondered why mentioning Willie Prentice's name acted like a burr under her saddle. Carlotta Dennison hadn't seemed the flighty sort. Slocum began worrying he had fallen into a sucking swamp he might never get free of.

He owed Ellen Garland for all she had done to get him through the empty prairie and patched up once they arrived in Fort Griffin, but he felt he owed her fiancé even more. He ought to get the pair of them together. Ellen wasn't the kind to imagine Willie Prentice had proposed to her. Why the raven–haired beauty's betrothed had hightailed it from Austin was beyond Slocum. Ellen was worth fighting for, and he didn't think too highly of Prentice, though he had never met him.

What connection did Lottie Dennison have with Willie Prentice—and Ellen Garland? And she had been frightened when Jack Porbaugh had accosted her. That Slocum could understand. The Jackal was aptly named. He could strike abject fear in the hearts of brave men. But Slocum had overheard him bawling out one of his cronies for even mentioning being sweet on Lottie.

Ellen Garland. Willie Prentice. Jack Porbaugh. They all circled round and round his thoughts as he pulled the balls from the keno goose. The work required no thought and Slocum found himself stewing something fierce by the time Curly came up to relieve him.

"Go on down and get a drink. You been doin' the work of three dealers tonight, Slocum."

"Thanks," Slocum said, anxious to take a break. His arm throbbed, but the pain had died. A shot or two of whiskey would remove even this small discomfort. As he went down the stairs, Slocum's keen eyes scanned the smoky room below for any sign of Porbaugh. He was feeling better, but he'd have to be a danged sight better before taking on his old trail companion.

"Good going, Slocum," congratulated Tom, pushing

over a shot of whiskey. Slocum sipped it and was pleas-
antly surprised. This had to be from the barkeep's private stock. It went down his gullet smoother than silk
and puddled warmly in his belly, not tearing at his in-
nards like a badger in a bag.

"Seen Lottie?" Slocum asked.

Tom shook his head. "Don't want to fire her. Have
to believe something bad happened and she's tendin' to
business. She ought to have let me know about it. I've
been askin' and nobody's even seen her around town.
It's as if she just upped and vanished like smoke."

"What of Jack Porbaugh?"

"You know The Jackal?" Tom shuddered. "I don't
fear many men, but he's a stone killer. I'm glad he
moved on."

"How's that?" Slocum perked up. "Porbaugh left
town?"

"The marshal got to snoopin' around, askin' questions The Jackal didn't want to answer. Don't know if
there's a reward out, but everybody in these parts knows
Porbaugh is rustlin' cattle. The fort's got a sizable herd
to feed the troopers. And there are a dozen other spreads
within a day's ride. That's a mighty powerful pull for
an outlaw like Porbaugh."

"And the herds are always a head or two shy when
they do inventory?" suggested Slocum.

"More 'n that," spoke up a cowboy next to him at
the bar. Tom hurried away to serve two buffalo hunters
banging on the bar, demanding an entire bottle of whiskey. Slocum saw how the barkeep added a drop or two
of nitric acid to each shot glass to give the whiskey kick
enough to satisfy the buffalo hunters' desert–strong
thirst.

"You know Porbaugh's a rustler for a fact?" Slocum
turned and looked at the weathered cowboy. He might
be in his twenties. He might be older. He probably
wasn't out of his teens.

"I work the Rolling Rock on the far side of the fort. Everyone in The Flats knows Porbaugh is stealing their beeves. Hell, we lost purt near two hundred head last month. The boss figgers they is over in Mexico and the gold from 'em is ridin' in Porbaugh's pocket."

"You wouldn't happen to know a gent by the name of Willie Prentice, would you?" Slocum wasn't sure why he asked. The question just leaped out.

The cowboy spat and hit the brass cuspidor squarely. He wiped his lips on the back of his sleeve. "Heard of the varmint. Jist a young kid?"

"That's him," Slocum said, not knowing what Prentice looked like, but he had to be about Ellen Garland's age.

"Works for my outfit. Jist hired on not a week back. Lazy as all get out." The cowboy knocked back the last of his whiskey. Slocum motioned to Tom to set up the cowboy with another shot.

"Much obliged. Don't often get free drinks just for spinning a yarn or two."

"Where's the Rolling Rock spread?" Slocum asked. "You said past the fort. How far?"

"A good hour's ride, if you have a fast horse. Three if you're goin' by buckboard. If you want to see Prentice, he's still out there. The boss only let those of us what been workin' come into town. Willie Prentice hasn't been on the payroll long enough." The cowboy turned his head and studied Slocum. "You have the look of a puncher. You huntin' for work? The boss was sayin' he could use an outrider or two. Pay's good. Forty a month and board."

Slocum showed the cowboy his broken arm. "Those are mighty fine wages," Slocum allowed. "I'd take you up on it in an instant, if I could do a day's work. Maybe in a month or so."

"Maybe," the cowboy said, turning to speak with another cowpuncher from the Rolling Rock. Slocum slipped away and went back upstairs, thinking hard. He wanted to find Willie Prentice as quickly as possible and discharge his obligation to Ellen. But leaving the Lost Dutchman now wasn't possible. The place was still crowded with customers, both for the bar and the gambling casino upstairs.

Slocum relieved Curly and went back to the dull job of turning the goose and calling out the numbers. Fewer men called for payoffs, and Slocum did little to encourage them. He even mentioned that Lottie wasn't likely to be back. When he did that, the gamblers vanished. Many had played keno only to while away the time until the popular faro dealer showed up for work.

Just past midnight, Tom sauntered up the stairs and cast an eye around the room. Two poker games at the far corner of the large room were the only action to be seen. He spat in disgust. He wasn't taking in any money from them.

"Need a couple tinhorn gamblers to work the room. Didn't think of hiring any whilst Lottie was here and drawin' in from all over The Flats. If she don't show up tomorrow, I reckon I'll have to find other ways of keeping the customers happy."

Slocum shoved over the thick wad of greenbacks he had hauled in from the keno game. Tom wrinkled his nose. Most of the bills had ridden in skinners' pockets and soaked up their stench.

"Expected more," he said, tucking the bills into a pocket. His eyes widened when Slocum reached under the table and dropped a leather pouch filled with gold dust and coins onto the table.

"My, my, you *have* been busy." Tom poked about in the pouch and smiled even more broadly. "This is 'bout the best night in weeks, and we done it without Lottie."

"Mind if I take off early?" Slocum was itching to get on out to the Rolling Rock Ranch and talk with

Willie Prentice. If he found a fast horse, he could be back before sunrise with word of the man for Ellen Garland.

"Go on, Slocum. Rest up. And here's a bonus for your work." Tom passed over four small gold coins. With the eagles, Slocum could buy himself a decent horse and some tack.

At that time of night it was difficult to find anyone willing to talk to him, but one stablehand forced open his eyes when Slocum held out the gold coins. This near the cavalry post too much of the money circulating proved to be greenbacks. Coin gave the stablehand the incentive to barter over a horse that was almost broken down and a McClellan saddle that Slocum knew would make his rump ache. But the price was fair enough for the time of night and what he bought.

Slocum fought to get the saddle on one–handed, then fought even harder to climb into the saddle. He settled down and the horse began crow hopping under him. Slocum took a few minutes to convince the old horse he knew how to ride, then started from The Flats, heading for Fort Griffin. The road was well traveled from the look of the deep ruts. He circled the stockade and found the smaller road leading toward the Rolling Rock Ranch.

He had been pushing himself too hard and almost fell asleep in the saddle as he rode, but the horse was content to keep moving at an easy gait. Slocum ought to have returned to Ellen's room and slept some. Tom expected him back at sundown to continue with the keno game. Making a long ride out to the ranch to talk with Willie Prentice only sapped his strength.

It also presented him with a way to ease his conscience. He had slept with another man's woman.

He rode, nodding off and jerking awake until sunrise. Slocum rubbed his eyes and saw a signpost indicating an even smaller path leading to the ranch house.

It took another half hour's travel before he saw the

bunkhouse. He heard chuck being called and licked his lips. His belly rumbled. He and food had been infrequent acquaintances, and the fragrant odor drifting toward him made his mouth water.

Pushing this distraction from his mind, Slocum knew the quicker he found Prentice, the sooner he could get back to Fort Griffin and a soft bed—without Ellen Garland in it.

"Howdy, mister," called a man with a stained white apron fastened around his middle. He wiped his hands and dropped a long iron rod he had used to call the cowboys to breakfast. "What kin I do for you?"

"I'm looking for Willie Prentice. Have a message for him from a lady friend."

The cook snorted and shook his head. "That one ought to keep his fly buttoned."

Slocum sat a little straighter in the saddle, aware of the strain on his rear and inner thigh muscles from the McClellan saddle. It was easier on the horse but hell on the rider, especially one still healing from a variety of wounds.

"You ain't comin' to call him out over some whore, are you?"

"Nothing of the sort. This is friendly," Slocum said. He hadn't even met Prentice and already he disliked the man. Ellen Garland deserved better than he was hearing about her betrothed. "A few minutes palaver is all I'm looking for."

"He got sent out on night herd."

Slocum laughed. It wasn't roundup time. Night herd was about the least favorite duty a cowboy could be assigned. Why anyone had been sent out to watch over the cattle on the open range was beyond Slocum.

"You know stock," the cook said, smiling crookedly. "That's more 'n I can say for Willie. Anyway, he's out there keepin' the rustlers at bay."

"One man?"

The cook shrugged. The cowboys came pouring from the bunkhouse, ready to be fed. "Got to feed this bunch of coyotes or they'll have my hide. I heard Willie's out in that direction. Can't tell you any more." The cook gestured due east, then swung around and hollered at the cowboys that he would throw out the food if they didn't get it down their slop chutes right away.

Slocum turned his horse's face toward the rising sun and started riding. He knew finding Willie Prentice would require quite a stroke of luck, but he had to find the man. Slocum had come this far. It wasn't going to do him or Ellen any good if he turned around and rode back to Fort Griffin.

To his surprise, finding the cowboy was far easier than he had thought. Less than a half hour out, he saw tracks leading over the grassy hills in the direction of a meandering stream used for watering. Slocum let his horse drink from the water. Slocum splashed water on his face and then dipped his bandanna in the stream, wringing it out and putting it around his neck. The heat was stifling. It would be another Texas scorcher.

Slocum's horse jerked back, tugging at the reins for no reason Slocum could tell. He knew the animal wasn't easily spooked. It was too easygoing. Leading the horse away from the water, he climbed a low rise. From here he heard what the horse already had.

"Gunshots," Slocum muttered. The sounds were quickly followed by the pounding of hooves. Slocum felt it through the ground and knew more than horses were running somewhere beyond his range of vision. A small herd, maybe a hundred beeves, had taken flight.

Swinging into the saddle, he groaned as he wiggled around. Then he saw the leading steers of the herd and knew they weren't stampeding because of a rattler or some sudden bovine urge. He couldn't make out the men, but at least three hurrahed the herd, getting them running toward the south.

A few more gunshots hurried the cattle on their way.

Slocum knew most of the Rolling Rock cowhands were back at chuck. To brazenly rustle cattle in the light of day amounted to nothing less than shameless disregard of authority.

He sat watching, counting four more rustlers. Slocum knew Jack Porbaugh had left Fort Griffin. Was this The Jackal's work? He couldn't be certain, but it had the man's brand all over it. Porbaugh had always taken risks far outweighing any possible reward.

Slocum knew he could do nothing to stop the rustlers. He studied the direction, got the lay of the land, and considered how long it would be to return to the Rolling Rock and fetch the cowboys. Unless Porbaugh ran the legs off the cattle, he couldn't get them far enough from the spread before the cowboys caught up with him. Even if they failed to catch the rustlers, they might get their steers back.

Tugging at the reins, Slocum got ready for the gallop back to the bunkhouse. A shot rang out, coming from quite a distance.

Slocum heard it, but his horse had already felt the effect. The horse snorted once and sagged to the ground, dead. Slocum rolled to keep from being caught under the horse's falling body. Staggering, he got his balance back and stared at the receding cattle being herded by the rustlers. Whether the shot had been aimed or was random, Slocum didn't know.

He did know it would be quite a hike back to the Rolling Rock. Slocum dusted himself off, then started walking.

9

Footsore and about tuckered out, Slocum walked up to the ranch house. Chuck was long over and the cowboys had scattered to tend to the chores around the ranch. The cook saw him coming and dropped what he was doing to come over.

"What happened to you?" the cook asked.

"My horse got shot out from under me by rustlers," Slocum said, more tired than angry by now. "I went hunting for Willie Prentice and ran afoul of maybe ten rustlers."

The cook swore and shook his head. "How long back was it? I didn't hear any shots."

"Close to an hour now," Slocum said. "You might get some men together and track the herd. The rustlers were heading due south from the stream with upwards of a hundred head of cattle."

"They'd be over onto the Triple Seven land by now.

We don't get on too good with old man Higgins. He's been known to tell his boys to shoot at us when we're running down strays.''

"Is he rustling your beeves?'' Slocum sank to the porch and brushed himself off. Clouds of dust rose and choked him. His feet were swollen and he sorely needed food and water. The cook wasn't likely to offer him any, not bringing bad news like this. Slocum reckoned he was lucky not to be shot.

"Higgins? Hardly. He's havin' trouble with them cow thieves himself. But he's cantankerous because that's his nature. Some men are jist like stepped–on rattlers, no matter what.'' The cook looked around as if worried someone might have overheard, then ran off to talk with a short, stout man with thumbs thrust into his belt coming from the bunkhouse. Among the punchers, this was the first one Slocum had seen wearing a six–shooter. The man's face turned into a storm cloud as he listened to the cook. Stamping his feet like a bull ready to charge, he came over to where Slocum sat.

"You the buck bringin' the news?''

"Depends on the news,'' Slocum said. "I saw rustlers out by the stream. They were herding close to a hundred of your cows.'' Slocum studied the man carefully and decided he didn't much like him. The man had the look of someone inclined to be vicious without cause, just because he could get away with it. Slocum had seen his like too many times.

"What makes you think they were rustlers?''

"If they weren't stealing from you, then you owe me a horse. Mine was shot out from under me. That's not neighborly behavior where I come from.'' Slocum saw shock at such insolence cross the foreman's face.

"What were you doing out there?'' The man turned more truculent by the minute as he realized he wasn't going to intimidate Slocum. His jaw set firmly and gave him the aspect of a bulldog ready to clamp his teeth into a victim. "You got any good reason for pokin' around on Mr. Royce's property?"

"Who are you?" Slocum asked. He was too tired to argue with the man. He thought from the way the man strutted around that he might be the ranch foreman. Wasting his time talking with anybody carrying a six–gun didn't appeal much to Slocum. He might end up with a slug in his gut.

"I'm Harriman, and you got a powerful lot of explaining to do."

Slocum said nothing, engaging in a staring match. Harriman backed down, but Slocum felt no sense of victory.

"My name's Slocum, and I came out here looking for someone. The cook was good enough to put me onto his trail. I happened across the rustlers, and they killed my horse. This is the last time I'm going to repeat this story. If you want to get after the thieves, do it. If you want to let them ride off with a hundred head of your steers, so be it, but it's on your head." Slocum pushed himself erect and shrugged his shoulders. There might be a muscle in his body that didn't protest, but he couldn't find it.

The old cavalry saddle had worn grooves in his butt, and the walk had jostled his broken arm, bringing back pain he thought long gone. Slocum wasn't in any mood to bandy words with Harriman or anybody else.

Pounding hooves caused all of them to turn and watch an older man galloping into the yard. The man's hat had fallen off and flapped behind him, held only by a leather strap circling his neck. Long white hair blew away from the man's weathered face. Slocum recognized a man used to power and using it. The Rolling Rock's owner had just discovered what went on out by his watering hole.

This had to be Royce.

"Get the men saddled. They're out there stealing our

beeves again!'' The bark of command caused Harriman to jump like a scalded dog. He started to obey, then froze. The foreman pointed in Slocum's direction but couldn't get the words out until he swallowed twice.

"Mr. Royce, this here varmint's just come in tellin' about the rustlers. I don't know what he—'' The foreman had no chance to rattle on. Royce rode over and glared down at Slocum.

"Who are you?''

"I came out here to talk with Willie Prentice,'' Slocum said.

"Prentice!'' bellowed the rancher. "I saw him riding with the damned rustlers. He's one of those thieving bastards! I gave that no–account a job, and this is the way he repays me!'' Royce dismounted and came forward, hands outstretched as if he wanted to throttle Slocum.

Slocum stood his ground and the rancher slowed when he bumped into his foreman. Royce turned and barked at Harriman, "Get the boys mounted. I want those owlhoots caught. I want those steers brought back. I want to see necks stretched before noon! Stop those rustlers!''

Harriman took off as if he had been shot from a cannon. Slocum ignored the foreman's rapid departure. He saw the cook edging away, returning to the safety of his kitchen. This wasn't part of his job.

"You're one of them,'' the rancher accused Slocum. He tossed his head and sent a banner of white hair fluttering in the hot wind blowing across the yard. When his hand went for the handle of the six–shooter at his hip, Slocum turned slightly, making it clear he could get to his Colt Navy before the rancher threw down on him.

"Don't go getting your dander up, Mr. Royce,'' said Slocum. "I lost a horse to those rustlers. I was trying to convince your foreman I saw the crime being done—I wasn't helping them steal any cattle—seems well nigh impossible."

"Willie Prentice," growled Royce. "You said you and him was pals. You're in cahoots with the rustlers!"

"Nothing of the sort," Slocum said, weary of the tirade. "I have business with him, and it's personal. If he's stealing your cattle, I know nothing about that."

"Get off my land," snarled Royce. "If you're not off my property in one minute, I'll see you horsewhipped!"

Slocum said nothing. He got down off the porch, knowing Royce was past reason. The rancher's cowhands had already mounted and formed behind their foreman. Harriman saw Slocum walking off and started to say something, then stopped when Royce bawled at him to get after the rustlers. The foreman spurred his gray and took off at a dead gallop, not sure what direction to go but going there full tilt.

Slocum coughed from their dust and wished them well. They were men pushed to the edge of tolerance by Jack Porbaugh—and Slocum did not doubt the rustlers he had seen were The Jackal's gang. It would take more than Marshal Ryder to bring Porbaugh to justice. It might take more than the entire troop at Fort Griffin.

Wearily putting one foot in front of the other, Slocum started the long trek back into The Flats. The ride out had been tiring. The walk back took every ounce of strength he had.

"Doc, can you fix up my feet?" Slocum asked, after trudging up the long flight of steps to Dr. Woodson's office. The giant chortled at seeing his patient return.

"I do declare, Slocum, you're going to make me a rich man. Climb onto the table, if you can." Woodson watched Slocum's weary steps with a practiced eye. When Slocum lifted his boots to the edge of the table, Woodson let out a low whistle.

"Don't usually see men accustomed to riding put

holes in the soles of their boots like that." He pried off Slocum's boots and tended the blisters Slocum had acquired getting back into Fort Griffin. "You ought to stay put for a spell and heal. If you keep up this pace, you're going to kill yourself." Woodson glanced up at Slocum and smiled widely. "Leastwise, you don't seem to be looking for others to do you in anymore."

"What's the difference?" asked Slocum. Relating his tale of being shot at by rustlers would serve no good. Slocum groaned as the doctor lanced the blisters and dabbed on disinfectant. By the time Woodson finished bandaging his feet, Slocum could hardly stumble along.

"I'll give you some advice for free, Slocum. Get new boots. My brother–in–law—this is another one, not the undertaker—runs a cobbler's store over on Second Street. Good prices. He might fix up this pair, cheap. Cheaper than I charge to patch your hide."

Slocum silently paid the doctor his due and noted how little money he had left. Leaving, he went directly to the cobbler's shop and got his boots repaired. The money he had left after paying convinced Slocum he had to spend another night working at the Lost Dutchman pulling keno numbers from the goose.

He stopped for a quick meal at a small café, then turned toward the Sam Houston Hotel. It was almost sundown, and Tom would expect him to show up for work promptly. Already, buffalo hunters filled the streets, whooping and hollering and getting ready for another night of blowing off steam. Besides, Slocum had nothing to tell Ellen Garland. He hadn't talked with her fiancé, and he didn't know for sure if Royce had been right in branding the man as a rustler. Until Slocum knew for certain what Willie Prentice was up to, he didn't want to burden Ellen with wild speculation.

Deep down, though, he didn't doubt the rancher. Prentice wasn't the kind of man who made a good husband.

"John, please stop, John!"

He took a deep breath and let it out slowly, trying to calm himself. Ellen Garland had found him. He hadn't wanted to speak with her until he could bring Willie Prentice along.

"Please, John, can we talk? I don't like you avoiding me like this. I haven't done anything to deserve your cold shoulder." The lovely dark–haired woman was close to tears. He pointed to a chair on the boardwalk.

"We can talk for a few minutes," he told Ellen. "Then I have to get to work. I've got a job at the Lost Dutchman."

"Why are you acting like this?" she asked.

Slocum wasn't going to get into the morality of what he had done. It was on his head, though Ellen Garland had been a willing participant. How willing he remembered with both desire and regret.

"I tried to track down Willie Prentice," he said. "I rode out to the Rolling Rock Ranch where he's working as a cowhand."

"You saw him?" Her joy burned away any remaining doubt Slocum had. She was in love with Prentice. Ellen grabbed his hand and pulled it close, to keep him from backing off. "How is he? Did you tell him I was in Fort Griffin waiting for him?"

"I didn't see him. I rode out and . . . and got shot at by a gang of rustlers," he said, not wanting to indict Prentice.

"Is he all right? Was he trying to stop the thieves?"

"I don't rightly know, Ellen. I didn't catch sight of him. I hightailed it back to the ranch house to tell the owner what I saw. He got together his hands, and they took out after the rustlers. I never saw Willie, and the rancher never mentioned any more about him."

"Oh," she said, folding into herself. Ellen sat with her hands folded in her lap, looking like a small child being punished for misbehaving in church.

"When the rustlers are caught, then it'll be a better time to find your fiancé," Slocum said, uneasy at Ellen's reaction. If she'd just come out and shout or cry, he could deal with that. Instead, she sat quietly, as if what had happened was all her fault.

"I don't know what to do, John. I love him, truly I do." She swallowed hard and lifted her face. Her blue eyes fixed on him. "I don't rightly know I don't love you, too, but not like I do Willie. Can you understand that?"

"I've had some practice," Slocum said, remembering too many other women who could never quite bring themselves to love a man like him. But Slocum knew Willie Prentice would do nothing but break Ellen Garland's heart.

"You get on back to the hotel. Room's paid up through tomorrow. We'll see then what we can do. The marshal might help," Slocum said, knowing the only aid the lawman would provide was a jail if Royce and his men caught the rustlers and didn't hang them from the nearest cottonwood limb. Chances were good Prentice would be among the number, if any were left for trial. The boy didn't seem smart enough to evade either the rancher or the law. And he sure as hell wasn't as vexatious as Jack Porbaugh.

"You will come to the room, after you've finished work?"

"I will," Slocum said, wondering if he told her a lie. He had no idea what Ellen had in mind, if he did go back to the hotel. He wasn't going to sleep with her again. Ellen Garland was spoken for, even if her fiancé might be a rustler working for Porbaugh.

"I'll wait for you. I want to know everything you've found out about Willie."

Slocum watched as she stood and quietly walked away, her tread more like she was climbing a gallows than going back to her hotel. There seemed no way Slocum could console her and not besmirch his own honor further. Rubbing his broken arm, he headed for the Lost Dutchman and another night of keno.

10

The keno balls rattled and clanked in the goose, then one tumbled out. Slocum called the number, trying to sound enthusiastic about it. The buffalo hunters seated at the table all whooped and hollered with every number, whether they won or someone else swept in a pile of chips. They sought only to drink themselves into a stupor and maybe get into a fight along the way. Gambling passed the time between falling unconscious and getting beat up.

When Carlotta Dennison came up the stairs, the room fell a trifle quieter as men turned and appreciated her dignified beauty. Then the noise rose and many of the players Slocum had kept happy for almost an hour went immediately to the woman's table. She smiled, but Slocum saw it was forced. Whatever he had said to spook her the night before still kept her on edge. Lottie waved

to him and then began shuffling the cards for the first
turn of faro that night.

Slocum wanted to talk with her and find what it was
about Willie Prentice that had sent her crying into the
night. Not enough of the clumsy gamblers left his table,
though, to let him take off. Now and then during the
evening, he saw Tom poke his head up the stairs, as if
assuring himself both his keno and faro dealers were on
duty. Seeing nothing out of the ordinary, the Lost Dutchman Dance Hall's owner had always retreated to tend to
the thirsty hordes below. Slocum drank slowly from a
small bottle he kept under the table and before midnight,
the pain in his body had died to an ache.

That was about all he could hope for.

Some time around twelve thirty the crowd of hiders
thinned out and a battle royal started downstairs. This
gave Slocum the chance to talk to Lottie.

For a moment, he thought Lottie would bolt and run
again. She settled down, controlling her obvious desire
to leave, and he approached her as he would a skittish
colt. If he'd had a lump of sugar, he would have held it
out to her, she was so jumpy.

"Evening, Lottie," he said, as friendly as he could
get. "I want to apologize for last night."

"No, John," she said quickly, hiding her embarrass-
ment with a quick toss of her head and a hand dragged
through her blond hair, as if combing it. The movement
settled her nerves enough to let her speak without seem-
ing more nervous than she was. "I ought to apologize
to you. It wasn't right for me to react the way I did."

Slocum paused, waiting for her to furnish an explanation of why she had acted that way. None came.

He had asked around about her and found out little.
Slocum began to see why. Lottie could answer a question and make people think it was all right, when she
hadn't said anything at all. When it came to revealing
anything about her life or thoughts, Slocum saw the

woman was expert at hiding everything. What black secret did she hide?

She went to church and she was as good a faro dealer as he had ever seen. But Slocum knew nothing else other than Lottie had come to Fort Griffin a few weeks earlier. Nobody knew where she lived, and unlike most women working in dance halls, she didn't socialize with the patrons. Not a single person had even hinted at her taking money for sexual favors. In truth, Slocum wondered if she enjoyed any male companionship. It didn't seem so from the way Tom and Curly kept their hopes unnaturally high regarding her affections.

"I'll buy you a drink when we're off," Lottie said, as if this would make all Slocum's questions vanish. She tilted her head to one side and studied him. "You look a fright. Are you hurting some?"

"Felt better in my day," Slocum allowed. His feet were worst of all right now, Dr. Woodson having patched up everything else the best he could. Slocum had to walk around and where he had blistered, his feet still burned as if he walked on live coals.

Lottie stacked piles of chips and moved them around, then looked him square in the eye. "You want to know about Willie, don't you?"

"Reckon so," Slocum said, knowing he wasn't going to get an answer. To his surprise she did tell him.

"He's an outlaw," Lottie said in a low voice. Slocum saw new sadness creeping into the woman's handsome face. She tried to put on a brave front, but Slocum knew the woman felt deeply about this. "He's only recently fallen in with bad company, but he's learning. Oh, how he is learning the ways of lawlessness."

"Cattle rustling?" asked Slocum. Lottie nodded slowly. Slocum knew he had to ask more, as much for his own curiosity as for Ellen Garland's benefit. Lottie had acted so out of character he had to know what it was that alarmed her so. "Did Prentice take up with the Jack Porbaugh gang?"

Slocum watched her carefully, but Lottie was an adept gambler. No sign of recognition flashed across her face when he mentioned The Jackal, but Slocum saw other telltale nervous twitches, ones she could not completely hide. Her finger tapped the table lightly, and she turned as if she wanted to move away a few inches. Nothing overt, but enough for a man looking for such a reaction. He had his answer, and it bothered Lottie even more because she knew she had given herself away. He began feeling sorry for her, and he didn't even know why.

"How did you come to know Willie Prentice? He's only been out at the Rolling Rock for a week or so. I don't think he's been in The Flats much longer than that."

"We've got to get back to work. The fight must be over downstairs." Lottie pointed. A half dozen skinners and two cowboys climbed the steps to the casino. One cowboy had a thick sheaf of greenbacks clutched in one hand and was bellowing how he wanted to break the bank. He had obviously won the money by betting on the right fighter and now wanted to parlay his windfall into a fortune.

"Come on over. You've got the look of a lucky man," Lottie called to him. Slocum knew he couldn't get any more from her. Their conversation had been brief, too brief, and he hadn't learned much more than that Carlotta Dennison knew Ellen's betrothed. But how? And what was Lottie's connection with Jack Porbaugh and his gang of rustlers?

Slocum returned to the goose and quickly began raking in money from the keno game. The men fanned out around his table were drunk with booze and the fight they had witnessed. Slocum tried to get some idea who had been battling below and then gave up. It hardly mattered. Two buffalo hunters had traded punches powerful

enough to drop a bull, and this had fired up everyone in
the Lost Dutchman by betting, cheering, shoving, and
drinking all the more heavily.

After two in the morning, Slocum's strength began to
flag. He had been through hell and knew he couldn't do
much more. Thinking he might convince Tom to let him
go early, Slocum saw something that sent energy surging
through his veins. He was dog tired, but Lottie had already closed down her faro table and was going out the
rear exit. He didn't think Tom or Curly knew, and that
made the lady dealer's departure all the more intriguing.

Slocum waited for a lull, then closed his keno rig,
fixing the goose so it wouldn't turn and putting the
money into an iron box held to the floor by a thick
staple. He snapped shut the lock and knew Tom could
fetch the night's take any time he wanted. Slocum went
to the rear door and stared into the night just in time to
see Lottie turning the corner half a block down the alley.

Slocum took the steps down two at a time, almost
falling in his haste. He slowed a mite to keep from div-
ing headfirst, then hit the alley and picked up speed
again. He chanced a quick look around the corner of the
building where Carlotta Dennison had turned and saw
her walking straight for a livery stable. Slocum followed
at a more leisurely pace, knowing she would spook and
run again if she saw him. But the woman was in a
powerful hurry to get to the stable.

He doubted she was going anywhere this time of
night. That meant she had a tryst. With Willie Prentice?
Slocum wanted to find out.

Lottie stopped outside the closed doors, shifting anx-
iously from one foot to the other, then pacing restlessly.
Slocum faded into shadows, content to wait and regain
some of his strength. He was beginning to enjoy the
pursuit. It gave him reason to forget all his aches and
pains.

When two men rode up, leading a third horse behind,

he sat up and strained to hear what was being said. Lottie marched over and began arguing with the men. Slocum couldn't get a good enough look at them, so he slipped along a wall, keeping in deep shadow until he was less than ten yards away.

". . . don't care what you say," Lottie raged. "It's not right. You can't do this. You can't!"

The woman's protests caused one mounted man to turn away abruptly, robbing Slocum of any chance of seeing his face clearly. Lottie stormed after him, reaching up and grabbing at his leg. The man tried to kick her away. Slocum's hand flashed for the Colt Navy at his hip, and he moved to leave his sanctuary in the shadows. He had the Colt Navy loaded again and could put a round through the mounted man's body if a good shot presented itself. It didn't.

Slocum stepped back into hiding when he saw that Lottie was in no immediate danger.

Lottie and the horseman exchanged more heated words, but the tenor of the argument changed. Lottie cooled down and began pleading with the man. The rider bent over and reached out for Lottie. She jerked away, then said something in a voice too low for Slocum to hear. Lottie let the man pull her up into the saddle so she blocked any chance Slocum might have had of identifying the rider. Lottie reached around the man's waist and rested her head on his shoulder. They trotted off, leaving the second rider and the spare horse.

Slocum relaxed and got a good look at the young man remaining behind. He dismounted and tethered the spare horse at a trough, then began making nervous gestures, as if he wanted to cut and run. When gunshots sounded down the street, the man jumped as if he had been the one shot.

"Willie Prentice," Slocum said under his breath. He had never seen the youth, but from Ellen's brief description, this had to be the lovely woman's betrothed. Slocum started for him when the youth vaulted into the saddle and galloped off.

Slocum stopped and stared. Prentice had not seen him. He had just upped and run because of the usual nocturnal activities in Fort Griffin. Slocum figured the gunshots came from a saloon where cavalry troopers or cowboys got a tad too drunk and decided to shoot up the place. The marshal would be out to put a halt to such frivolity before long.

"The marshal," Slocum said, wondering if that was the root of Willie Prentice's uneasiness with staying behind in The Flats. If so, this confirmed that the stripling rode with outlaws and had a guilty conscience about his activities.

Slocum took a few steps in the direction taken by Carlotta Dennison and the other horseman and knew he could never find them. But the fleeing boy was another matter. He kicked up a large cloud of dust a blind man could see. If he thought to elude the law, he was doing a pisspoor job of it.

And then there was the spare horse. It stood quietly, occasionally bending down to drink from a nearby trough, then straining to reach a bale of hay nearby. Why it had been brought, Slocum didn't know, but it presented him a sterling opportunity. He had lost one horse to rustlers. If Willie Prentice rode back to the campsite of The Jackal's gang, that meant this horse had probably come from there.

"They owe me a horse," Slocum said, running his hand over the animal's rump. The saddle's leather was stiff with neglect, but the horse appeared strong and able to run all night. Slocum pulled himself into the saddle, sighing in relief. This was no McClellan saddle tormenting his hindquarters. It hadn't been properly cared for, but Slocum didn't mind.

Pulling up the reins, he turned the pony's head in the direction taken by the running Willie Prentice and took off after him. Slocum kept up a canter until reaching the outskirts of Fort Griffin. He saw his quarry made no attempt to hide his trail. The boy stayed on the road and raised such a ruckus Slocum would have had to be both blind and deaf not to stay on the trail.

Not once did the rider slow, stop to survey the land, or find out if anyone followed him from town. He knew where he was going and went there straight as an arrow. Slocum fell back a ways, not wanting to get too close, since the youth had to be nearing the rustlers' camp. If Prentice and his companion had ridden into The Flats as the boy rode out, the camp couldn't be too far away.

Slocum's hunch proved accurate. The man he thought to be Willie Prentice suddenly veered off the main road, went down the step embankment of a gully, and vanished from sight. Slocum reined back and let his stolen horse walk to the verge. There, he dismounted and studied the rocky arroyo bottom. Even in the darkness he saw evidence that more than a single horse had come this way recently.

"Might be ten riders or more," he said softly to himself when he saw how cut up the arroyo was. A slow smile crossed his lips. He knew he was nearing the end of his hunt. Finding a way down into the ravine proved difficult, since he didn't want to use the same rocky path Willie Prentice had taken. If he approached the rustlers' camp, they'd have guards on duty. Riding into a leveled rifle muzzle wasn't something Slocum wanted to do.

Slocum found that his horse wanted to go down immediately, more proof that the outlaws were near. The horse sensed the camp as its home and wanted to return, to grain, currying, better care than Slocum was giving it.

Dismounting, Slocum let the horse have its head, and he followed it, slipping and sliding down the pebble-strewn slope. He tumbled into the arroyo, recovering in a hurry and catching up the horse's reins. Slocum dragged out his six-gun and listened hard in case any of the rustlers had heard him. Nothing disturbed the stillness of the Texas night. In the distance, a lovesick coyote howled mournfully and a soft breeze caressed the creosote bushes. No significant sound came to his attentive ears.

Walking carefully to keep from turning his ankle on the fist-sized stones littering the bottom of the ravine, Slocum let the horse precede him. The horse snorted and tried to jerk free several times. When the scent of burning mesquite reached him, Slocum tugged at the horse's reins and drew it to one side. He tethered the horse securely and advanced on foot.

To his disgust, he found only a spot where Willie Prentice had climbed the bank and ridden off across the prairie. Slocum heaved a sigh, returned, and got onto his horse. He put his spurs to the animal's flanks, urging it ahead faster than before.

The horse clambered up the slope and took out across the prairie. Slocum had lost sight of the other rider entirely. And as quickly as he had decided to ride again, so did Slocum find himself in the center of a dozen men.

Their campfire had died out, leaving behind the lingering odor of mesquite he had smelled only minutes before. Slocum had thought their camp would be farther off from the way Prentice had been riding, but he had been wrong.

Slocum stared down and found a dozen rifles and six-shooters pointing up at him. He had nowhere to run.

11

Slocum cast around for some way out and saw nothing. Foolishly, he had not paid attention and had ridden into the middle of a camp filled with outlaws. And not a one of them looked as if he'd let Slocum ride away without filling him full of holes.

His hand twitched slightly, trying to move toward his six-shooter, but Slocum knew he would be dead on the spot if he made any move for his Colt. Forcing his hand to remain at his side, he looked down on the men and tried to hide his consternation at his mistake.

"Evening, gents," he said, settling forward in the saddle to cover his slight movement and keeping his voice level. Slocum's eyes danced from man to man, trying to find Jack Porbaugh. If The Jackal was in camp, Slocum knew he was a dead man. Some of the others might have been with Porbaugh when he confronted Slocum before, but everything had happened quickly back in the saloon.

Slocum had to hope the men didn't recognize him.

If not, he would be pushing up posies.

"If Willie Prentice is here, I'd like a word with him."

"You ain't the law?" The question came sharply, and Slocum knew he was halfway home. If the owlhoot holding the rifle aimed straight at his head was the least bit inclined to think he was a marshal, Slocum knew he would have been dead already.

"Don't hold much for lawmen," Slocum said. "Had my troubles with them in the past. Reckon I will again in the future." He fixed his gaze on the man and stared hard. Slocum wasn't surprised when the man didn't back down, but he was downright relieved when the rifle swung away.

"What you wantin' with Willie? He ain't done nothing to speak of."

Curiosity. They were curious, and that kept Slocum alive a few seconds longer. Several more six–guns lowered as the men came closer to hear the answer. Slocum relaxed even more. He wasn't out of the woods yet, but he had a glimmering of the way to go.

"This is personal. I don't have a feud with him. I've got a private message to pass along from a lady friend who is real interested in seeing him again."

"Willie, a lady friend? He couldn't find a whore if he had twenty dollar bills stuffed up his rear! What's she like, this woman of his? A real dog?" This sent a ripple of laughter through the camp. More guns slid back into holsters. Slocum saw only a pair of rifles trained on him, probably from men supposedly on guard duty.

He let himself chuckle, too. "She's not the best–looking woman in Texas, but she's not so bad—if you've been on the trail for six months following behind the herd."

This got the last two rifles pulled off him. Slocum knew they could turn on him again at any instant, but for the moment he was as safe as if he was in bed.

Slocum swallowed hard at that thought. He wasn't all that safe, because he had been in bed with another man's woman. He wasn't sure what he was going to say to Willie Prentice, but he had to come up with something that didn't rile the boy up and get him to flinging lead in all directions.

"How'd you find us, mister?" A tall man, skinny as a rail, walked over from the cook fire and squinted at Slocum. "Nobody knows we're here. Nobody." Slocum saw the men around the campfire tensing up again, ready for action.

"Jack and I go back a ways," Slocum said. There was enough ring of truth in his words that his inquisitor shrugged it off. Jack Porbaugh had quite a history and his men assumed others did, too. Slocum's luck held and none of the men in Porbaugh's gang had ridden with him—and Slocum—over in New Mexico.

"Willie's out there in the corral, tending his horse. He jist rode in. You followin' him from town?"

"Came from over at the fort," Slocum lied. "They're mad as wet hens over someone stealing their cattle."

This provoked a round of deep laughter, and Slocum knew for a fact he had found the rustlers. There hadn't been a lot of question in his mind, but now he knew and that made it even harder for him to get out of their camp. Somebody might take it into his head that Slocum was a witness to illegal activity and decide to use him for target practice. The tall, thin man had the aspect of a gent willing to kill his own grandmother, if someone offered him more than two bits to do it.

"You want me to go find him?" Slocum asked, still wary.

"Go on out, mister." The thin outlaw stood with his hand resting on his holstered six-shooter, still not sure if he should draw or go back to the plate of beans he was eating. Slocum hoped he didn't think to ask names. Claiming acquaintance with both Porbaugh and Prentice might come back to haunt Slocum. The Jackal would find out quickly who the visitor had been and blow up like a keg of blasting powder.

Slocum urged his horse through the camp and dismounted at the far side, aware they watched him. He knew now how a mouse felt when stalked by a tomcat. Not turning or showing any distress, Slocum walked slowly until he reached the crude corral formed by a half dozen mesquite bushes and a few ropes. Willie Prentice worked on a horse, haphazardly currying it.

"Prentice?" called Slocum. "Can I have a word with you?"

"Who's there?" The young rustler came over and stared at Slocum, not knowing him. "Do I—"

"I got word from Ellen," Slocum said quickly, knowing the others would be eavesdropping. Being a rustler meant being wary, especially of strangers claiming to know someone in the gang.

"Ellen!"

Muffled laughter from the direction of the camp told Slocum he had been right. The rustlers were listening to every word he said to the young outlaw.

"She's back in Fort Griffin. The Flats, actually, not the fort itself. She came up here to find you."

"She shouldn't have gone and done a fool thing like that," Prentice said in exasperation. He took off his hat and whacked it against his leg. "I tole her I'd be back before she missed me."

"She missed you real quick. Why'd you come out here from Austin?"

"Ellen really sent you? Are you a friend of hers?"

"And a friend of yours, though you don't know it. Your other friends are all interested in the intimate details of your courtship with Ellen." Slocum jerked his thumb in the direction of the rustlers' camp.

"Come on over here," Prentice said tiredly, taking Slocum's arm and pulling him into the makeshift corral.

Louder, Willie Prentice shouted, "You git on back and mind your business. This isn't none of your concern."

Laughter from the shadows told that most all the rustlers had been spying. This reaction from Prentice took away any hint of trouble. Footsteps faded as they returned to their camp, joking and laughing at their youngest member.

"I tole her I'd make it big, then I'd marry her. Ellen's got no call followin' me here. This is no place for a lady!"

"You figured to steal enough to win over her father?" Slocum had heard all the stories before. He just hadn't thought Willie Prentice was stupid enough to believe he could steal money sufficient to convince Ellen Garland's father that he wasn't a ne'er–do–well. Men like Ellen's father who had made piles of money recognized only hard work and possibly even honesty. Prentice thought to find a quick way to riches and avoid the hard work necessary to earn his own.

"Why not?" Prentice thrust out his chin and tried to look defiant. He wasn't old enough to make it work. He ended up feeling uncomfortable under Slocum's scrutiny. Willie Prentice turned and went back to his currying.

"I ain't never had anything to speak of, not like Ellen. Her family's not real rich, but they're well off. I can't offer her anything less than that. I can't!"

"She wants to marry you. She doesn't much care if you have money."

"I do," Prentice said, turning sullen. "I want to give her everything she's growed up knowing, and there's no way in hell I can do that without a thick wad of greenbacks ridin' in my pocket."

"You have a trade? Blacksmithing? Farming? Those are the ways to make money."

"Who *are* you?" demanded Prentice. "I ain't seen you before. You ain't tryin' to push me aside so you can have Ellen for yourself?''

Slocum fell silent for a moment. The young man hit mighty close to the target with that shot. Slocum had been thinking how easy it would be to turn Willie Prentice over to Marshal Ryder—or any of the ranchers Porbaugh's gang preyed on—to get rid of the young man. Ellen might have a fondness for him, but he was hardly more than a boy. Slocum was a man and could offer Ellen Garland far more.

He sucked in a deep breath and let it out. He had been brought up an honorable man. He might have slept with Ellen, but she wasn't his woman. She had come to Fort Griffin hunting for Willie Prentice. Slocum knew she wasn't likely to want any other man for quite a spell if something untoward happened to Prentice. Ellen would go into a decline and return to Austin, losing herself in the bosom of her family. Depending on her affection for Prentice, she might never take a husband and die a spinster.

The times they had spent together were all Slocum was ever going to have with her, no matter what happened. If she and Prentice got together, a wedding looked to be the logical thing to happen. If Prentice was killed, either in a fight or by having his neck stretched by a lynch mob, Ellen would go into mourning. And if her beau landed in prison for a good long time, she might do some damnfool stupid thing like pine away waiting for him to get out.

''I owe her for saving my life,'' Slocum said, stating the truth as simply as possible. ''You want to know more, you ask her. I promised her I would track you down, and I have. What's next is up to you.''

''I can't see her. Not yet. Not until I've made my stake. When I have a pile, we can go west and buy good land.''

''You a farmer?''

Slocum saw no answer on the man's face.

"A rancher? You like stealing beeves. You know anything about raising them?" Slocum knew then that Prentice had no trade. Slocum didn't come out and say it, but thieving might be all Willie Prentice was good for.

"Don't come after me with those questions. You sound like Ellen's pa!"

"Come on back to The Flats with me. It's still dark and you can get in and out of town before sunrise."

"I ain't afraid of anybody seein' me," Prentice said sullenly.

"You can be back to your rustling before any of the men in camp miss you." Slocum hesitated a moment, then had to ask, "How'd you come to know Jack Porbaugh?"

"We met in a saloon. He said he was lookin' for a few good men and recognized my sterling qualities. I been doin' good since I tied up with him. I set up the steers we stole off the Rolling Rock." Prentice was bragging now, and Slocum didn't like it. Porbaugh played him for a fool, and Prentice never saw it. If the law came looking for anyone, it would be Willie Prentice from Austin, not The Jackal from parts unknown.

"Don't bother with the details," Slocum said, knowing the young man hadn't done too good a job. Everyone on the ranch recognized he was responsible for the rustling. Willie Prentice was lucky if there wasn't already a bounty put on his head.

"I can go back into town with you. Or you can tell me where she is. I'll talk to her and pound some sense into her head."

"What?" The coldness of Slocum's question froze the boy in his tracks.

"I didn't mean it like that. I'd never hurt Ellen. She means more to me than anything else. All I meant to say was I'd talk her into going home. Fort Griffin is a hellhole compared to Austin."

"Let's ride," Slocum said, growing aware again of

eyes boring into his back. He swung into the saddle and cast a quick glimpse around, trying to find who watched him. Slocum didn't see anyone, and that made him even more uneasy.

"All right. I just got in from town. If I'd knowed she was there, coulda talked with Ellen then." Willie Prentice began muttering to himself as he worked on his horse.

Slocum waited impatiently as the youth saddled and got ready to ride again. Prentice rode back into camp and talked with the tall, thin outlaw for several minutes. The argument died down, and the man waved Prentice from camp.

This easy agreement put Slocum even more on edge. It wasn't in a suspicious man's nature to let riders come and go from bivouac. There would be at least one tracker on their heels. And if Slocum had been in charge, there might be more.

"You're mighty uneasy. There a good reason?" Prentice swung about in the saddle to scrutinize Slocum more carefully. "You ain't some kinda bounty hunter after my scalp, are you?"

"What I told you about Ellen was true. If I was the law, there'd be a posse all around me." Slocum held up his broken arm.

"Might be a trick. Jack told us about some of the dangedest things bounty hunters have tried to catch him. They never have. He's never been in the calaboose one single day of his life."

"And The Jackal's a damned liar," Slocum said, knowing Porbaugh had been in the Silver City jail. That was the reason Porbaugh had come after him with such a vengeance back in Fort Griffin.

"Don't go callin' him names," Prentice said hotly. "The man's gonna make me rich. He knows more about—"

"Quiet," Slocum snapped. He heard hoofbeats, more

than could be attributed to just one horse. "Would they follow you?"

"The guys back in camp? Why would they? I'm one of 'em," Prentice said proudly. Slocum wanted to shake him until his teeth rattled. What did Ellen see in this wet–behind–the–ears boy? Cooling down, Slocum realized he was letting his feelings for Ellen color his opinion of Willie Prentice.

"They mostly have rewards on their heads," Slocum said. "The people they consort with would turn them in for anything more than a plugged nickel." He tried to get his bearings and failed. Leaving the road might not have been a good idea, he now realized. Still, Slocum preferred heading across the prairie to riding smack–dab into an ambush. He wasn't sure if the riders he heard came from town or from the direction of the rustlers' encampment.

"What are you doing?" Prentice asked.

"We'll split up. You keep riding a ways and let me fall back to see who's behind us. If it's all right, I'll catch up. Otherwise, you light out for Fort Griffin and see Ellen."

"All right," Prentice said, not sure of Slocum or the plan.

Slocum wasted no time in wheeling his horse and backtracking. He was only glad that Prentice hadn't recognized the horse as the one he had led into Fort Griffin earlier. Prentice was not overly observant. But Slocum began to think he was running from shadows when he rode back a half mile and found no trace of pursuit. He knew all the tricks of tracking and couldn't have missed even a lone rider after them.

Turning in a full circle, Slocum slowly realized his error. The sounds he thought had been coming from behind were actually ahead of them on the trail. He put his heels to the horse's flanks to catch up with Prentice and warn of the trap. The young rustler was riding head-long into trouble.

Before he had galloped a hundred yards, Slocum heard gunshots. He went cold inside. Slocum knew he was responsible for the young man's life. Keeping low over the horse's neck, Slocum made as good a time as he could getting back to where they had parted ways, then going beyond.

A low rise saved him. He heard another gunshot and loud voices, angry ones shouting incoherently. Slocum reined back and slid from the saddle, advancing on foot. He fell to his belly and watched the play on the other side of the hill.

It made him catch his breath and hold it. Willie Prentice was circled by a half dozen men with leveled rifles and shotguns. The riders he'd heard weren't from Porbaugh's gang.

Marshal Ryder and five deputies had caught Prentice, and there wasn't a damned thing Slocum could do about it.

12

"String 'im up, marshal," a man demanded stridently. Slocum slipped along the sandy ridge and dropped flat on his belly when he saw two of the men shift in the saddle and turn in his direction. He recognized Harriman from the Rolling Rock and the man speaking had to be Royce. His shock of white hair billowed from under his hat, though Slocum couldn't see the man's face clearly.

"We're not a lynch mob," Ryder said angrily. "We caught the man you claimed stole your cattle. A jury will determine if he's guilty and—"

"*If!*" roared Royce. "There's no if about it. He's the one who done the deed. Him. Willie Prentice. I'd recognize that damned sidewinder anywhere. He and his gang has stolen beeves from every spread in central Texas. And ask Captain Stanley at the fort. He'll want this varmint, too!"

"I'll be sure to let the fort commander know we

caught him, Royce,'' the marshal said, ''but we got to get together a jury and—''

''Why bother getting a jury? There're enough of us here to hold a trial. I say he's guilty. What about you, Harriman?''

Royce got the answer he expected from his foreman. Slocum rolled onto his side, winced, and drew his six-shooter. If Ryder lost control of his posse, Slocum would have no choice but to try to stop the lynching. He owed Ellen Garland something, and it wasn't herding her betrothed into the hands of a mob intent on making him do a midair dance.

To Slocum's surprise, Ryder showed some backbone. The marshal drew his rifle, cocked it with great fanfare, then laid it across his saddle, finger curled on the trigger.

''Don't make this worse than it is, Royce. We caught him. Now we try him fair and square. Then we can hang him.''

Slocum realized this was the best Prentice could hope for. He sank back down, wondering what Prentice might say about his companion. One mention of anyone riding with him and the posse would pick up the search again, and Slocum wasn't in any condition to get away if they came for him.

To Slocum's relief, Prentice fell into a sullen silence. Whether he thought he was being brave by not betraying Porbaugh and his gang, or if it never occurred to the boy, Slocum couldn't say. Whatever the reason, Slocum was glad for it. The posse got Prentice moving back toward The Flats, arrayed around him to prevent any escape.

Sliding back down the sandy hill, Slocum went for his horse. Riding on out and not looking back seemed more appealing all the time. But Slocum couldn't do that. It wasn't his fault Prentice was going to jail, but he hadn't discharged his obligation to Ellen Garland. If Prentice kept quiet about everything, Slocum might find a way to get him out of the town's dingy cell.

Slocum rode back to the main road and paused again, the hard decision before him. Riding away from Fort Griffin and never looking back was the course of a coward, and Slocum was not that. Ever. What he would tell Ellen about her boyfriend danced in front of him, only to slip away like a greased pig. There had to be the right words, but Slocum couldn't decide what they might be.

"When in doubt, find someone who might be able to give the answer," he said to himself. He returned to Fort Griffin, intent on seeking out Carlotta Dennison. She knew a great deal about the Porbaugh gang. She had been the one to tell him Prentice rode with the rustlers. If Slocum could get more from her about the gang, a deal might be worked with the marshal.

"Porbaugh traded for a young buck not even wet behind the ears," Slocum said, turning the notion over in his head. It sounded good to him. Marshal Ryder ought to go for it, too, since Porbaugh had bounty money riding on his head that would far exceed anything to be paid for Willie Prentice.

Slocum rode into The Flats and immediately found a flaw in his plan. He didn't know where Lottie lived. A slow smile crossed his lips as a different plan formed. He knew the one person in town who might know where the mysterious lady gambler lived. As if the horse had ridden toward the church every Sunday, the animal trotted over to the tall steepled structure. A single light burned at the rear. The parson put in long hours, since it was still several hours before dawn.

Dismounting, Slocum stretched his sore muscles and went to the side door. He knocked and the parson answered immediately. The man obviously expected someone else, because his eyebrows rose in surprise at seeing Slocum.

"Can I help you?"

"I need a favor," Slocum said. "It's real important

that I find Lottie Dennison. A friend of hers is in trouble, and she's in the best position to help out.''

''Are you Mr. Slocum?'' The question startled Slocum. He stepped back a half step and studied the parson. If he had crossed trails with him before, Slocum didn't know when.

''I am,'' he said slowly.

''Lottie has mentioned you and your helpfulness.'' The parson sighed and chewed on his lower lip for a moment. ''I am sure she would have let you know where she lives if she had meant,'' the clergyman said, ''but she also said you did not lie. If you say it is a necessity to find her right away, it must be.''

The parson hastily scribbled on a piece of paper and thrust it into Slocum's hands. ''Here's a map. It's out of the way but not that hard to find. She likes her privacy. Will you respect it?''

''Of course,'' Slocum said, glancing at the map. It didn't surprise him that Lottie's house wasn't far away. He touched the brim of his battered Stetson and jumped into the saddle. Slocum rode fast and found the small adobe house exactly where the map indicated. Slowing to a halt, Slocum stared at the house and wondered if his idea was good. Carlotta Dennison had no reason to help out Willie Prentice. Or did she? Slocum knew so little about her.

What had the meeting in town earlier been about? Prentice had come in with another man, who had ridden off with Lottie. There had been an argument, but she had left of her own will. And the spare horse had been for her. Slocum patted the horse's neck. Prentice and the other rustler had come into The Flats intending that Lottie leave town with them. Instead, she had ridden out behind the second outlaw.

''Lottie!'' he called, not wanting to get too close. Slocum had the feeling she might come to the door and open up with that derringer of hers. Or she might still

have a visitor—the man she had ridden off with earlier.
"It's John Slocum. I need a word with you."

He waited a minute and took a deep breath, wondering
if he ought to leave. A lamp shone through the window
and he saw movement inside the small adobe. He dismounted when the door opened. Lottie stood there, rubbing sleep from her eyes. She didn't have a gun in her
hand, and that counted as a win for Slocum.

"What is it? I reckon Mr. Trenchard told you where
I lived."

"The parson? It was," Slocum acknowledged.
"Don't hold it against him. I need some help."

"You? Help?" Lottie laughed and the sound was mu-
sical. Slocum had to smile.

"It's Willie Prentice. The marshal caught him."

"Willie?" Lottie's amusement vanished. "Come on
in, John. It's still mighty cold out here." She went into
the small house. Slocum followed and found a place that
was exactly the way he thought it would be. Neat, clean,
with only a few pieces of furniture, this was a sanctuary
more than a place to spend a life. Lottie was running
from something and had come to light here, just for a
while, before moving on.

"What can I do? I've only known Willie for a short
while, but I recognize much in him that—" She bit off
the rest of her sentence. "What can I do to help him,
John?"

"He needs someone of good character to speak up for
him. I don't think Royce has a case against him, other
than suspecting him of rustling from the Rolling Rock
herd."

"He did steal those cattle," Lottie said. "I know he
did. I can't testify any other way, John."

"Then don't," Slocum said. "But he needs someone
to watch over the trial to be sure Royce doesn't railroad
him. I overheard how he wanted to stretch Willie's neck.
The boy doesn't deserve that. He's gone wrong, but he

might be put back on the straight and narrow.''

"Possibly. He talks big, but he isn't the outlaw the others are.''

"The ones like Jack Porbaugh?'' asked Slocum, watching her closely. Color came to Lottie's cheeks.

"Yes, like Jack Porbaugh,'' she agreed. "I'll dress and go into town. I think I know why you can't do this, John.'' Lottie went to a small chest and began pulling out clothing.

Slocum knew it was time for him to go. "Much obliged, Lottie. I hope this isn't for nothing.''

"Trying to save a wayward soul is never the wrong thing to do,'' she said, venting a deep sigh as if the weight of the world rested on her shapely shoulders. Lottie dropped her clothing on the small bed and came over to the door. She placed her hand on his stubbled cheek and stared into his eyes.

"You are a hard man, John Slocum, but there is a goodness to you, too.'' She kissed him lightly, startling Slocum. He didn't know what to do or say.

"Go on, find Prentice's young woman and tell her what's happened. We can talk after I've seen Marshal Ryder and found out how serious this is likely to be.'' Carlotta Dennison turned from him, and Slocum knew it was time to go.

As he mounted, he felt a fleeting sense of loss. Seldom did he leave a place and feel this way. As he rode into The Flats, Slocum came to realize it was Lottie who affected him most. She was one hell of a woman, different from most he met.

Slocum rode slowly, still not wanting to confront Ellen Garland with the news of her boyfriend's capture. She had to know he was going bad—or at least suspect. Why else would he hightail it from Austin and come to a place with Fort Griffin's unsavory reputation?

Nearing The Flats, he saw more activity around the jail. Slocum knew he should fetch Ellen and let her talk

with Willie Prentice, but something was going on that
Marshal Ryder was finding hard to cope with. The lawman stood in front of the jail, his rifle held high. When
he fired into the air for silence, Slocum saw that the
posse had turned into a lynch mob backed by half the
population of the town.

"Hush up!" Ryder shouted. "You don't have any call
being here. Go home, have a good breakfast, go about
your business. Let the law enforcin' fall to me."

"You're holding a criminal, marshal," someone in
the crowd shouted. "We got a witness. He's the one
who killed Doc Bond."

Slocum's ears pricked up at this. He rode closer, staying mounted to get a better view of the crowd. He
couldn't tell who was calling out about Bond's death.

"He killed everyone on that stagecoach. He's a robber
and a rustler!"

"Bring the witness out where I can talk to him," Ryder said. Slocum's eyes narrowed when a man came
from the crowd, a broad grin on his face.

"I saw it all, marshal. He's the one who killed the
driver and the passengers. He robbed the stage. I'll testify to that in court."

Slocum started to speak up, then clamped his mouth
shut. The only people in any position to know were Ellen Garland and John Slocum—and Slocum had not
seen this fellow before. Other than the survivors from
the stagecoach, only the outlaws who had held up the
stage would know who had pulled the trigger on Doc
Bond.

"He's guilty!" someone shouted. "Hang him. Don't
bother with a trial. Why waste our time?"

"Because he is guaranteed that under our laws,"
came Carlotta Dennison's loud voice. "I don't know if
he robbed a stagecoach. It doesn't matter what *I* think,
anyway. Or any of you. It matters what a jury thinks.
He deserves that much. Why are you all in such a pow-

erful hurry to hang him? If he's guilty, what's a week or two more?''

"Get on out of here. And you," Ryder said, pointing to the man who had accused Prentice of the robbery and murder, ''get into the office so I can talk to you.'' Ryder hesitated when he almost ran into Lottie. She stood her ground. The marshal touched the brim of his hat and went back inside the jail without saying a word to her.

Slocum started to ride to the Sam Houston Hotel and Ellen Garland but stopped and stared. He wondered at Lottie's quick appearance in front of the jail. He hadn't run his horse into the ground getting here, but she must have well nigh killed hers to arrive so quickly. The lady gambler had not passed him on the road, so she had cut across the prairie, coming into town from the south.

He sat and watched as she turned and hurried off on foot. She hadn't seen him. Slocum considered going into the marshal's office and adding his two cents concerning witnesses to the stagecoach robbery, then decided finding where Lottie went in such a hurry was more important. He walked his horse along the street, in no hurry to catch up with her.

Somehow, Slocum wasn't too surprised when she returned to the stable where she had met Willie Prentice and the other man hours earlier. Getting down, Slocum hitched the horse and entered the alleyway leading to the stables. His hand jerked toward his Colt Navy when he saw who Lottie met.

Jack Porbaugh.

The rising sun cast a beam of sunlight between buildings that shone on the outlaw's face. In the morning light The Jackal didn't look like a wide-eyed killer. Slocum knew different.

He pressed into the splintery planking of a building to keep from being seen. With the light in Porbaugh's eyes, there wasn't much chance, but Slocum didn't want to hazard it. He would have shot the man down like a

mad dog if Lottie hadn't been standing next to him. Slocum strained to hear what they said.

He couldn't. But what he saw turned him cold inside.

Porbaugh reached out and grabbed Lottie. He pulled
her to him and kissed her hard. Slocum didn't see the
woman doing much in the way of resisting. If anything,
Slocum thought she was returning the kiss. Porbaugh
pushed her away and only then did the woman have
anything to say.

"Jack, please. Don't do that."

"You didn't do much to discourage me, Lottie. Then
again, you never did."

Slocum frowned. Lottie was as chaste as anyone in
Fort Griffin—maybe the most righteous. No one had
said a word about her being with any man while she had
been in The Flats. She was a moral woman and one who
had dealings with a notorious outlaw.

Porbaugh threw his arm around Lottie's shoulder and
drew her into the stable, cutting off any chance Slocum
had of hearing what they said. He started forward to get
a better position when he heard the neighing of horses.
He chanced a quick look around the corner of the building and caught his breath. If he had run out without
paying attention to his surroundings, half of Porbaugh's
gang would have seen him. And cut him down like a
stalk of wheat.

Slocum considered his chances, then decided he had
to get to Ellen with the news of Willie Prentice's capture
before she heard it from someone else. He didn't like
leaving Lottie with The Jackal, but the woman didn't
seem to be in any danger. Snorting in disgust, Slocum
realized her situation was as far removed from danger
as could be.

Strides lengthening, Slocum left the alley and hurried
down the street toward the hotel and the unpleasant task
ahead of him.

13

For all his resolve, Slocum slowed when he reached the hotel lobby. Stopping dead in his tracks, he started dreading his chore. The stairs leading to Ellen's room might as well have been the thirteen steps leading to a gallows—with Slocum the guest of honor. He cast a quick glance in the direction of the room clerk and saw the man hadn't stirred since the last time Slocum had passed through. If anything, the snores were even louder than before.

Slocum knew he had to grasp the nettle and pull hard, no matter how much it hurt. He deliberately mounted the steps up to Ellen's room and knocked softly, hoping she wouldn't be in. It took several seconds before Slocum heard her moving inside the room and almost a minute more passed before she opened the door. The dark–haired woman stared at him with her wide blue eyes and a look that made him want to cut and run. She had nothing but hope written on her face.

"John! You're back. Did you find him? Did you tell Willie I was in town?" She grabbed him and dragged him into the small room. Slocum felt uncomfortable here. He couldn't keep from remembering the night they had spent locked in passion on this bed. Sitting on it, pretending there was nothing between them, was hard. If anyone had pressed him on it, Slocum would have been forced to admit he had feelings for Ellen Garland. She was lovely, spunky, and appealed to him more than any other woman for a long time.

Telling her about her betrothed and not sounding the least bit happy pushed him to the limit.

"What's wrong, John? You couldn't find him? Oh, I worried that might happen." Ellen sank onto the bed beside him, her hands clenched in her lap. She wore a long, chaste white cotton nightgown, but it clung to her trim figure and caused Slocum a minute's uneasiness.

"It's not that way at all," Slocum got out. "I found him, and the news isn't good."

"What?" Her blue eyes widened in surprise. "Tell me. You have to tell me, John. No matter what's happened, I can take it. I must know what's happened to Willie." She looked so apprehensive, Slocum knew he had to finish the tale. Anything less and Ellen would go crazy with worry, not that she wasn't likely to fret over Prentice's arrest.

"He's fallen in with a gang of rustlers. They're vicious men and keeping up with them meant committing crimes. I don't know he's actually killed anyone, but I know for a fact he's rustled more than a hundred head of cattle from the Rolling Rock."

"But he was working there. Willie would never steal from anyone generous enough to give him a job!" Ellen's eyes widened in surprise that Slocum would invent such a tall tale.

"He got the job to round up the cattle for Jack Porbaugh. The Porbaugh gang is raiding every ranch in the area. They've even stolen some steers from the cavalry.''

"Oh," she said in a small, choked voice. "I worried he would have turned to crime. He wanted to make a lot of money so we could get married. That didn't matter, but he wouldn't listen to me. He's all that matters to me, John. I love him more than anything else. Why has he done this? Why?''

"I believe you, and I tried to tell him that money didn't count with you." He held up his hand to forestall her outpouring of questions. "Yes, I talked to him. I even got him to ride back into Fort Griffin to see you.''

"He's here? In town?''

Slocum tried to think of a way to sugarcoat the news and couldn't. "He's in town, all right, locked up tight in jail. A posse caught him out on the prairie. Marshal Ryder wanted him for rustling, but it's turned worse than that.''

"What? How could it be any worse?''

"Someone's come forward claiming to be a witness to Willie holding up the stage and killing Doc Bond.''

"What's that? I don't understand. We were the only ones to get away alive and—''

"Exactly," Slocum said. "It might be one of the gang who held up the stage, or it could be someone with a grudge against Prentice. Whichever way it is, he's got murder and robbery charges leveled against him, too.''

"I can testify that Willie wasn't among those holding up the stage. You can, too. You know he wasn't there. You said you talked with him. You can tell the court . . ." Ellen's voice trailed off.

"I don't know if he held up the stage or not. I might have been the shotgun messenger, but I can't identify any of them. He could have taken part in the robbery, but I don't think so.''

"One step at a time," Ellen said, coming to a conclusion. She wasn't going to abandon her fiancé, whatever the charges. "We get those charges removed, then worry about the cattle rustling."

"He did that crime," Slocum said. "There's no question. Royce, the owner of the Rolling Rock, knows. His foreman does, also. And there are other people Willie told. He's bragged to enough folks so everyone knows." Slocum's thoughts turned to Carlotta Dennison. Had Porbaugh told her of the boy's involvement, or did she know firsthand Willie Prentice was a rustler? The lady gambler held the cards for this turn. Depending on how those cards were played meant the difference between life and death for Prentice.

"I must talk with him. Where is he? The jail?"

Slocum nodded. He saw Ellen go to a small wooden chest and open it. Several new dresses lay inside. She had used the money he'd given her to replenish her wardrobe.

"I'll see what can be done. I'll meet you at the marshal's office when you get decent," Slocum told her, moving toward the door. Slocum paused, wanting to say more, but there was nothing more he could tell her. Truth was, Slocum could hardly take his eyes off her as she rose from the bed and began selecting her garments. Ellen Garland tried to look unconcerned, but her courage was flagging quickly in the face of overwhelming evidence against her boyfriend.

"Willie is lucky in one respect," Slocum said, settling into a chair at the rear of the Beehive Saloon. "The circuit judge might have taken a month or longer to get to Fort Griffin."

"Some luck," grumbled Ellen. She sat beside Slocum, hands folded in her lap as if she prayed for Prentice's release. Slocum knew it wasn't likely to happen. Prentice had been jail only three days before the judge had ridden into town on his long-eared mule, but the crowd gathered outside the jail had kept up a steady chant for those three long days, fed as much by the cowboys from the Rolling Rock as by any desire for real justice.

The people in The Flats had seen their share of lawlessness from gamblers and buffalo hunters and the cavalry troopers, and a little rustling hardly amounted to much. But the witness against Prentice claiming the youth had killed Doc Bond turned most of the town out against Prentice. The stagecoach driver had been popular in town, having kinfolk living nearby. His stories about nursing most of the townsfolk through a cholera outbreak proved true, too. Everybody cried for justice, no matter that the witness was a lying son of a bitch—or worse, one of the real robbers. Nobody wanted to listen to Slocum, in spite of his being shotgun messenger on the stage.

Folks refused to listen to Ellen, too. Slocum was sorry that she had ever let it slip that she and Prentice were engaged. The people of Fort Griffin claimed she wanted only to get her boyfriend out of jail and would do anything, including lie for him.

"We can get this over with real quick," the judge said, sitting down behind a couple of planks thrown over the backs of two wooden chairs. He took out an old six-shooter and rapped the butt sharply on the table until it vibrated with the blows. Louder he called, "Settle down, y'all. We got a trial to hold. You the defendant?" The judge peered nearsightedly at Willie Prentice.

"He is, Your Honor," spoke up the prosecutor, a man who looked more like a prairie dog than a human. His round button nose twitched, and he rolled his shaggy brown-haired head about so his jowls bounced. Twin eyes the color of coal peeked out, adding to the image of a prairie dog hunting for danger.

"Where's Willie's lawyer? The one I hired?" asked

Ellen. She looked around, not seeing the lawyer in the ersatz courtroom.

Slocum shook his head, then sat a little straighter in his chair. Prentice's lawyer came in the Beehive's side door. From the way he staggered, he was drunker than a peach orchard sow. Flopping hard, he crashed into his chair. If Prentice hadn't grabbed him by the arm, the lawyer would have fallen to the floor to sleep off his load of whiskey.

"That your mouthpiece?" the judge asked, still squinting hard at Prentice. "Good. We're all here and can get started. Jury's seated," the judge said, nodding in the direction of twelve men chosen at random by walking along the town's main street and asking for jurors. "Everybody get quiet now. Start presentin' your evidence."

The prosecutor gave a weak case, but Slocum watched the way the jury ate it all up like ants going after a filled sugar bowl. More than one reached into a pocket to surreptitiously draw out a flask. A quick pull or two of liquor, maybe passing the spirits around to neighbors, then the bottle disappeared into a coat pocket. Before the prosecutor had gotten halfway through his case, the jury was as drunk as Prentice's lawyer.

"They're railroading him," Slocum said angrily. "There's no way this court will let Prentice off." He sat and stewed. He knew Willie Prentice was guilty of rustling. But to convict him of a crime done by someone else—and murder, to boot—was wrong. The prosecutor worked more on the murder and stagecoach robbery charges than anything else.

"When we're called, we can set them straight," Ellen said, lying to herself.

"What makes you think we'll ever testify?" Slocum asked, bristling. The prosecutor had one witness, the gent who had accused Prentice. He wasn't likely to hunt for evidence destroying his case. And Prentice's lawyer was so cockeyed drunk he kept falling out of his chair. Remembering his own name, much less which witnesses to call on his client's behalf, eluded him.

Carlotta Dennison entered the Beehive and sat on Slocum's far side. He saw the storms of indignation building in her, too. Lottie glanced at Ellen and then reached out to reassure her. Ellen stiffened, not sure who this was.

"They've got him convicted already," Slocum said to Lottie. "Is there anything you can do?"

Lottie shook her head. "I can tell the truth, but I am not going to be called as a witness." She smiled ruefully. "What is there I can testify to? Willie's good character?"

"We can't let this happen!" raged Ellen Garland. "Why—"

"Hush," said Slocum. He stood and watched as a heavy iron box was dragged into the courtroom. "That's the strongbox from the robbery. Where'd they find it?"

The top had been blasted off and the contents taken. Slocum hadn't expected anything less. But recovering the box amounted to a miracle. The outlaws who took it could have abandoned it anywhere in Texas between Fort Griffin and the Rio Grande.

"Would you tell us, Marshal Ryder, where this was found?" The prosecutor beamed at his witness. The marshal cleared his throat and started in on a tale Slocum would have bet was rehearsed like some play at a nickelodeon.

"I rode out to where Prentice camped. I got his bedroll and other gear. As I was leavin', I happened to see something shiny. Pokin' around, I unearthed this here box. Mr. McGrath identified it as belongin' to the Abilene Stagecoach Company."

"The same company who lost a stagecoach to outlaws? The same company whose driver, Leonard Bond, also known as Doc Bond, was killed? Is that correct, Marshal Ryder?''

''Reckon so,'' said the marshal.

The buzz through the saloon told Slocum that Prentice had no chance. His lawyer never stirred to object or raise a point in his client's behalf. When it came time for cross-examination, the lawyer blathered and blundered, making himself a laughingstock.

''That does it,'' Slocum said. ''There's no way Prentice can get off on the murder charges.'' Seething, Slocum realized what conviction really meant. Willie Prentice would be held responsible for the robbery and the law would stop looking for the real outlaws. Someone had committed four murders and robbery and would get away scot-free.

Slocum could only wonder if the robbery had been planned by Jack Porbaugh. The Jackal always had an eye for the easy way out. Saddling Willie Prentice with the crime was that and more. It let Porbaugh continue rustling and pillaging for a few days longer, and every day without the law breathing down his neck added more cattle to his rustled herd.

''I was wrong. The road agents who held us up aren't in Mexico. They stayed close by. And they want to do some more robbing and killing.''

Slocum turned to Lottie to ask about her and Jack Porbaugh. He was the only one likely to have committed the robbery, the murders *and* the rustling.

''That about does it, Your Honor,'' said the prosecutor, brushing his hands together as if he had finished a dirty chore. He chuckled when Prentice's lawyer tried to rise to object, only to slip and bang his chin on the table as he fell. The prosecutor struck a pose and declaimed, ''If there's nothing else to be said, why not let the jury go decide what's to be done with this . . . miscreant?''

The judge rapped for order and said, ''We can have

this over and done with 'fore noon, if 'n we hurry. Why don't you fine gentleman go on into the back room and talk it over?''

The foreman of the jury shot to his feet and shouted, ''Ain't no need for us to go set a spell, Your Honor. Me and the boys all agree. That son of a bitch is guilty!''

''On which of the charges?'' asked the judge. He began scribbling in a small notebook beside his six–gun.

''Everything. He done everything they said he done. Now, kin we hang the bastard?''

That sentiment met with the general approval of those assembled in the saloon. Men stood and jeered, grabbing for Willie Prentice. The marshal moved to protect his prisoner but didn't seem too anxious to do a good job of it. More than one fist landed on Prentice's face and body as the angry townspeople shouted at him.

Ellen Garland buried her face in her hands and began sobbing, then shot to her feet and raced from the saloon.

14

"They can't do this," muttered Lottie Dennison. "It's a complete miscarriage of justice! And it's just like Jack to send one of his men to lie on the stand!" She swung about in her straight–backed chair and saw Ellen outside the Beehive Saloon, crying her eyes out. Lottie shot to her feet and stormed from the room to comfort the younger woman. Slocum remained seated, knowing what was going to come. He was glad the women had left.

The judge banged the butt of his six–shooter on the rattling wood planks and barked, "Hush up, y'all. I got to pass sentence on this varmint. Boy, stand up." The judge glanced from Willie Prentice to his notes, then said in a clear voice, "You've been found guilty of killin' a popular, law–abidin' citizen. No reason to pussy-foot around on this. I sentence you to hang by the neck till you're dead, dead, dead. I hereby order the marshal of this town to carry out the sentence no later than sun-down today.''

A cheer went up. A few gasped and then sighed in relief. Most were pleased at the verdict and capital sentence. Life had been dull in Fort Griffin lately and this livened things up a mite. Slocum sat for a moment, composing his thoughts. He realized he was in a small town and most thought Willie Prentice had murdered Doc Bond. Bringing a killer to justice counted for much.

Whatever Willie Prentice's crimes might be, murder wasn't likely to have been one of them. Not during the stagecoach robbery. And if Prentice had been one of the eight robbers attacking the stage, no one but another robber could ever truthfully accuse him of the crime. Slocum saw the sole witness against Prentice smirking. The man accepted a round of thanks from many of the townspeople, then took a free drink when the bar opened again.

More than his obvious lying, the man had been in-dicted as being one of Porbaugh's gang by Carlotta Den-nison. That testimony meant nothing, however, in the face of public opinion. Unless Slocum did something, Porbaugh would see Prentice swinging for a crime he didn't commit.

Pushing through the crowd, Slocum went to talk with the judge. The small man shoved his six–gun into his holster and gathered a few items he had scattered on the crude table. His notebook vanished into an inside coat pocket and he tucked a larger law book snugly under his arm. He started from the saloon until Slocum blocked his way.

''How can I help you?'' The judge looked Slocum over. His watery eyes worked up and down, lingered for a moment on the worn ebony butt of the Colt Navy, then fixed firmly on Slocum's cold green eyes.

''He's not guilty. Not of murder. I was shotgun messenger on that stage. Another passenger and I should have testified for him.''

"That was up to the boy's lawyer.''

"He was drunk and you know it,'' Slocum said coldly. "He was so drunk the damned shyster couldn't even sit up without Prentice holding him erect.''

"Reckon so, but the boy had representation. That's what the law says got to be done. You're not going to cause trouble over this, are you? We got laws against that, too.''

"Prentice is a rustler, not a murderer. Why should he rob a stage when he's been busy stealing other people's cattle?''

"So you'd rather have him rot in Huntsville for five years than get his neck stretched?'' The judge muttered to himself and shook his head. "I'm not sure which is more merciful. You ever seen Huntsville?''

"Justice isn't being served, Your Honor. The men who really shot down Doc Bond, the other passengers, and the depot manager are still riding free out on the prairie.''

"So, get Ryder to deputize you and change that. Or run for sheriff. I understand Shackleford County is in search of a new sheriff. John Larn isn't too interested in bein' in that office again.''

"I don't want to enforce the law,'' Slocum said. "I just want justice done.''

"Can't say I cotton much to my job, son. Become a judge. I'll give you my circuit. The pay's pisspoor, and I spend all my time riding a swaybacked mule. Can't even afford a decent horse and buggy. And it's been almost a month since I sat down with my wife and family for a home–cooked meal.''

Slocum saw he was getting nowhere. He grabbed the judge by the arm when the man started out of the saloon again. "Wait. Prentice didn't get a fair trial. The witness against him—''

"What about him?" demanded the judge, jerking free of Slocum's grip.

"The only people at the killing, other than Miss Garland and me, were the outlaws doing the robbing. He never said how he came to witness the murderers or why he didn't help us out. Men died because we didn't have enough guns aimed at the road agents."

"He should have been asked those questions on the stand. He testified fully and he was sworn in, so I have to assume he was tellin' the truth. Anything else would be a crime. Perjury. Your friend's lawyer didn't ask the right questions. Hell, he didn't ask *any* questions, but Willie Prentice was represented. Now, if you don't let me go, I'll have you clapped in the darkest cell in the Fort Griffin jail for contempt of court. I got to be over in Fort Worth by this time tomorrow and there's no way in hell I'm going to make it on that shiftless mule." The judge stalked off.

Slocum watched in amazement. The judge knew Willie Prentice had been railroaded and yet did nothing about it. As far as he was concerned, because Prentice had a lawyer, even an incompetent, drunken one, justice had been served.

"Wait a minute," Slocum said, rushing after the judge. "Jack Porbaugh's the one responsible for the robbery. I can't prove it, but he's been rustling cattle in these parts for the better part of a month. What's a stagecoach robbery to him?"

"Porbaugh?" The judge arched one eyebrow and scratched his chin. "Reckon he's enough of a buzzard to do something like killing Doc Bond, but there wasn't evidence presented to cast doubt on young Prentice's part in the robbery and murder."

"I don't know if Porbaugh was there, but he might have been. He's a more likely suspect than Willie Prentice." Slocum wondered what argument would sway the judge. He saw this wasn't the one that would do the trick.

"Can't argue that," the judge said. "Would you feel any better if I authorize a hundred dollar reward on Porbaugh's head? I keep hearin' his name. Figure he's done something illegal or so many people wouldn't be whisperin' about him so much."

"No, it wouldn't make me feel any better," Slocum raged. "Prentice is going to be executed in less than ten hours for something he didn't do."

"Begging your pardon, son," the judge said tartly. "A jury of his peers said he *did* do the deed. Accept the reward on Porbaugh's head as the best I can do. The rest is in the strong hands of the good citizens of Fort Griffin—and God." The judge stretched, yawned widely, went to his mule, and mounted. The lop-eared beast protested under the small judge's weight and then started walking out of town, heading toward distant Fort Worth.

Slocum spun and went off in search of Carlotta Dennison. She knew where Jack Porbaugh was. He had seen them together, and the lady gambler hid more than she revealed. It was time Slocum found out a bit of what Lottie already knew. But Slocum couldn't find her. He hesitated to go to the hotel and see if Ellen knew where the other woman might be. Sitting and commiserating with her wasn't what was needed. Action would save Willie Prentice, not talk and tears.

He stopped at the Lost Dutchman Dance Hall and yelled over at Curly, who idly cleaned glasses while waiting for men from the trial to come in for serious drinking.

"You see Lottie today?" Slocum asked.

"Nope, not a hair of her lovely head. Should I tell her you're lookin' for her? I thought you and her was supposed to be at Prentice's trial."

"We were. Need to find her right away." Slocum saw Curly shrug and knew he couldn't waste any more time hunting for Lottie. He had to find the Jackal and bring him in. Nothing less would be acceptable to Marshal Ryder.

Even then, turning over the man responsible for most of the crime in the county might not save Willie Prentice. But it couldn't hurt.

Slocum checked his six--shooter and rubbed his broken arm, trying to keep down some of the itching in it. He knew this meant his busted bone was healing, but it distracted him more than outright pain. He stood on the boardwalk in front of the Lost Dutchman and scanned the dusty street from one end to the other. At the far end of town, people went about their business.

And at the other end, out near the cemetery, a dozen carpenters worked to build a gallows. Slocum forced himself to look away from the half–built structure. He didn't see Lottie anywhere and hunting for her would only waste time. He knew where Porbaugh's gang had camped the night before. Picking up their trail wouldn't be too difficult and from there he could find The Jackal. After that, Slocum knew he would have one whale of a fight on his hands.

"On my hand," he corrected himself ruefully, shifting his weight to relieve a bit of strain on his left arm. Over the years Slocum had been busted up plenty, but seldom had any of the injuries slowed him down much. The only good thing about his broken arm was that it was his left, not his right. Having his gun hand all wrapped up would make any real effort to help Willie Prentice futile.

Slocum jumped into the saddle and turned his stolen horse to head out of The Flats. He rode steadily, the sun beating down on him and causing rivers of sweat to drip into his eyes. Worst of all was the way his bandaged arm itched. The heat and the healing both did it, but Slocum couldn't ignore the sensation. He spent a goodly part of the ride out of town scratching madly.

On the road he urged the horse to greater speed. This got him to Porbaugh's campsite faster and forced him to keep his hand on the reins and away from his left arm. The terrain flowed smooth and flat, with only a few ravines and rolling hills to relieve the boredom. When Slocum found the gully he had tracked Willie Prentice across the night before, he slowed and studied the ground.

"Damn," he said with feeling. The ground was chewed up enough to show an entire cavalry company had ridden through recently—but the direction was wrong for the troopers, if they came from the fort. Porbaugh had struck camp and moved his men. There wasn't any reason for Slocum to search the abandoned camp now. Besides, unless The Jackal had salted the evidence elsewhere that had condemned Prentice, the camp would be barren of evidence to use.

Slocum needed Jack Porbaugh in the flesh and talking a blue streak, not a few flimsy clues that could be interpreted any of a dozen different ways.

In a way, Slocum's luck ran high. He saved himself the ride to the old camp. He turned to track the fleeing outlaws, hoping they hadn't gone too far. From the length of stride of their horses, Slocum knew they hadn't been galloping. A slow, deliberate retreat might mean they were simply moving to another spot nearby. He rode cautiously, remembering how he had fallen into their midst by accident four nights previous.

"Got you," Slocum said after an hour of tracking. He saw a stand of pin oaks and a few cottonwoods near a watering hole. Horses wandered about on short tethers, enough horses for this to be Porbaugh's gang. All Slocum needed was continued luck—and for Jack Porbaugh to be in camp.

Dropping to the ground, Slocum staked his horse in a gully and moved to see who rested in the camp. The hot Texas sun wore him down, but Slocum ignored it. He had to get Porbaugh back to Marshal Ryder before sundown or Prentice would be dancing on thin air.

The sound of hoofbeats forced Slocum to drop flat and wait. Not ten yards distant rode the man who had testified against Prentice. He wobbled in the saddle, clear indication of how much free liquor he had drunk back in Fort Griffin.

"Hey, Jack, Jack, I'm back!" yelled the false witness.

Slocum used the furor caused by the man's approach to get closer. A small stream ran past the stand of trees. Slocum got to the far side of the creek and duckwalked through obscuring weeds until he got within earshot of the gang's encampment.

Slocum parted the spiny growth and watched as Jack Porbaugh swaggered over to talk with his henchman.

"What's the verdict?" Porbaugh demanded. "If it's anything less than hangin', I'll have your ears cooked up for lunch."

"Prentice's due to swing at sundown. They're buildin' gallows just outside The Flats."

"Good, good. That'll take the heat off us for a few more days. By then, we'll have finished with the Rolling Rock herd and gotten on down to the Star Bar X spread. That'll give us a herd of damned near a thousand head. We're gonna be rich when we sell 'em down in Mexico, boys."

This was greeted with loud cheers. Slocum knew the drive from central Texas to Mexico would be long and treacherous, but the rustlers didn't care how many head reached the Rio Grande alive. All the cows were stolen, not painstakingly raised to turn a profit. Even if Porbaugh got only three dollars a head, a herd that large meant a considerable wad of greenbacks—or gold—riding in his pocket.

"You got Prentice taken care of all good and proper?" Porbaugh asked.

"Surely did, Jack. He's not gonna open his trap 'bout us, either. He's got all kinds of silly notions of loyalty that he'll die with."

Porbaugh laughed again and slapped the man on the back. The pair of them wandered off in the direction of a stand of trees screening them from the others. Whatever business The Jackal had to talk over, Slocum wanted to hear more of it.

He made his way along the creek, careful not to be seen. Most of the rustlers drowsed in the heat. Only two of them meandered around, possibly guards, but more likely just restless in the heat. Slocum crossed the running water and dropped to his belly behind a fallen log. Not ten feet away Porbaugh and the witness against Prentice talked in guarded tones.

"We don't need 'em, Jack. Let's just take the cattle and go," the man urged.

"We do need them, leastwise till we get to Mexico. Why split the take from the beeves with all of 'em?" Porbaugh laughed and it wasn't pleasant. "I done paid back Lottie for her takin' up with Prentice like she did. That'll teach her to try to shoo off my men, even fools like Prentice."

Slocum knew Porbaugh would never play straight if there was a dime's profit in treachery. He had double-crossed Willie Prentice. Cowboys from the surrounding countryside would flock into Fort Griffin to see the execution. Now he wanted to steal from his own gang, maybe thinking up some way to turn them over to the law for rewards or just leave them dead.

Slocum wondered what mischief Porbaugh planned for the ceremony—or during it. The bank might be left unguarded. Or did he simply want the region's attention turned toward The Flats and away from protecting the herds? Whatever crime he plotted, Jack Porbaugh would be gone in a few days unless Slocum stopped him now.

Drawing his six-shooter, Slocum knew a single shot would end the outlaw's life. But that accomplished nothing but Slocum's own death. He would be run down by the others in the gang before he could get halfway back to his horse. More than Porbaugh's death, he needed the rustler to confess and clear Prentice's name of the Abilene Stagecoach Company deaths.

A slow smile crossed Slocum's lips thinking on that. He would pay back Porbaugh, if he could get him to Marshal Ryder—and it would repay Lottie Dennison, too. Porbaugh carried a big hatred for her because she had tried to get Prentice to go straight, from the sound of the outlaw's complaints.

"Go on, get another drink. Relax. The real work's ahead of us tonight," Porbaugh said to his henchman.

"Aw, Jack, you know how I hate ridin' night herd."

"I know how you enjoy spendin' money. Think of all the whores you can buy with your share. Get on back." Porbaugh slapped the man on the shoulder again, then sank down to draw diagrams in the dirt. Slocum wished he could see what the outlaw drew, but the angle was wrong and bushes got in the way.

Moving through the undergrowth, Slocum found a game path. If Porbaugh came this way, he'd follow the path. Slocum looked around and found a sturdy oak tree. He had a devil of a time climbing up it with his broken arm, but he finally lay flat on the thick, low limb over the game trail.

Then he whistled, low and shrill. The sound wouldn't carry far—not much farther than Jack Porbaugh, Slocum hoped. He drew his six-shooter and pointed it at the path. When Porbaugh came underneath him, he'd have the drop on The Jackal.

Slocum heard footsteps, slow, muffled, hesitant. He whistled again to draw the outlaw into his trap. From his vantage on the limb, Slocum couldn't see the path, but it didn't matter. He heard Porbaugh coming closer.

"Come on, you son of a bitch," Slocum said between clenched teeth. Porbaugh was a cold–blooded killer. Slocum knew he could never plug him and get away with it, but he could slug Porbaugh to keep him from calling out for help. It would be hard getting the outlaw away from his camp, but Slocum knew it had to be done. Without a show of daring now, Willie Prentice would be doomed at sunset.

Porbaugh stepped on a twig and signaled that he was almost under Slocum's perch.

As Slocum readied himself to drop down and buffalo Jack Porbaugh with his pistol barrel, a voice rang out clear and loud. "Hey, Jack. We got something to show you."

Slocum cursed when he heard nothing more indicating approach. He swung over the limb and fell hard to the narrow dirt path. His Colt Navy swayed back and forth—nothing. Jack Porbaugh had retreated, going back to his camp.

Throwing caution to the winds, Slocum hurried along the path, intent on putting a bullet in Porbaugh's head, no matter what it would cost him. When he heard the thunder of horses' hooves, Slocum broke into a dead run. To Slocum's disgust, he got to the rustlers' camp and found it empty. Porbaugh and the rest of his gang had mounted and ridden off.

Slocum's best chance for capturing the rustler had passed. He peered through the leafy canopy formed by the trees and saw the sun sinking past the zenith. There wasn't any chance of him tracking Porbaugh down now and getting the outlaw back to town before Willie Prentice was hanged.

Slocum reluctantly went to his horse and headed back

to Fort Griffin. There had to be some other way of saving Willie Prentice. What it was, he didn't know. But he'd have to think of it quickly. Prentice had only scant hours of life left before his execution.

15

Dejected, Slocum rode back into The Flats. The activity
there struck him as outrageous, even for a town cele-
brating the victory of law over the lawless. People
crowded the streets, but Slocum noticed right away that
work had stopped on the gallows. A cold knot formed
in his gut as he put his heels into the horse's flanks,
urging it forward.

He reined back near the marshal's office. A large
crowd outside told him something was wrong. Bad
wrong.

"What's going on?" Slocum called down to Curly.
The barkeep shook his head and came over to Slocum.

"I don't know how to tell you this," Curly started.
"It's pretty damned bad."

"Spit it out," Slocum snapped. He wasn't in any
mood for the barkeep to dance around the truth. "What
happened?"

"Dead," Curly said, head shaking even more. "Hard to believe, but it's so."

"Prentice? He tried to break out?" Slocum realized this might be for the best. Better to die with a bullet in the belly than a hemp necktie cracking the neck.

"No, Slocum, it's not Prentice I'm talking about. It's the little lady, your friend. The one you—"

"Ellen?"

"That's the one," Curly said. Tom came over and chased the barkeep back to the Lost Dutchman.

"I wish he had softened it a mite before telling you," Tom said. "The girl tried to bust him out of jail. She didn't know what she was doing."

"She's dead?" Slocum didn't feel cold or angry. He didn't feel anything. It was as if he had simply turned hollow inside. All he had done for Ellen Garland amounted to nothing now. She had saved his life, as he had saved hers. For what?

"The marshal didn't have much choice. She busted in waving a six-shooter around. She got off a shot or two. One bullet almost took Ryder's head off. He drew down on her. He's not much of a lawman, but he's a good shot. Or maybe just lucky. He hit her smack-dab in the heart with his first round."

"What about Prentice?"

"He never saw her. She never got past the marshal's office. He's still scheduled to swing at sundown. Looks like more folks will turn out now. You know how people can be. Morbid curiosity. They'll want to see how Prentice takes the news. Don't know if he's heard or not, being locked up an' all."

Slocum wasn't listening to Tom's maundering. He tugged on the reins and got the horse moving away from the jail. Shouts and sights and smells vied for his attention. He just rode, not knowing where he went. He couldn't believe that Ellen Garland was gone, snuffed

out in the prime of life. She had been so alive, so vital—
and now she was dead.

Before he reached the outskirts of Fort Griffin, a smoldering rage began warming him, making his blood rush
faster and burning away the lethargy of shock. Ellen
Garland had been too good for the likes of Prentice. She
had deserved more, better. And now she and her lover
would be buried together in the town cemetery.

Slocum found himself heading for Lottie Dennison's
house without knowing why. He reined back and stared
at the adobe. Anger burned higher in him, rage at the
judge and Porbaugh's henchman who had lied to get
Willie Prentice into jail and at Ellen for doing something
so stupid. She had no idea how to cope and had reacted,
thinking only to save the man she loved.

"Lottie!" Slocum called twice before the woman
came from the house. She stared at him, a stricken look
on her face. She knew what had happened.

"John, come on in. We need to talk." She motioned
for him to enter the small house. Slocum swung down,
his rage burning away all the pain in his body. He entered the coolness of the house and felt some small
measure of serenity just being near Lottie.

"I heard what happened," Lottie said, sitting on the
small bed. "I'd tried to calm her down, but there was
no consoling her. But please believe me, John, I never
thought she'd get a gun and try to break him out."

"She walked in and thought the marshal would let
him go," Slocum said. "Ellen didn't have a chance."

Silence fell between them. Slocum felt the currents
flowing back and forth, though, powerful ones. He had
lost Ellen forever, but she had never been his. Not really,
since she belonged to Willie Prentice. And some loss
also saddened Lottie.

"Who is it?" he asked her. "Who have you lost? And
what hold does Jack Porbaugh have over you?"

Lottie turned stricken eyes to him, then burst out cry-

ing. Slocum didn't know what to do. His own anger had
cooled. He knew the only way he could strike out and
feel any better would be to bring The Jackal to justice.
Jack Porbaugh ought to be sentenced to the gallows, not
Willie Prentice.

And not Ellen Garland. She hadn't deserved to die.

"Sorry," Lottie said, trying to stop her sobbing. She
dabbed at her eyes, then felt around for a handkerchief.
Slocum saw one lying atop her clothing chest and
handed it to her. Their fingers touched. Slocum started
to pull back, but Lottie gripped his wrist with strength
borne of need. She tugged hard enough to get him off
balance. He took a step and then another and knew he
was being pulled into a whirlpool beyond his control.

He sank down beside her on the bed.

"We shouldn't do this," he said.

"We should," Lottie corrected. "We have to, John.
I need it. So do you." She leaned over and tentatively
kissed him. He didn't respond. "We have to forget, if
only for a moment. Please, please, John. Help me forget,
and I'll help you."

She kissed him harder. This time he felt himself melt-
ing inside. Slocum returned her kiss with mounting passion. She crushed her firm body against his. He felt her
lush breasts compressing and poking into him. They
sank back onto the small bed, Lottie's fingers working
to get his gun belt free.

They kept kissing and turning and stroking over each
other's bodies. He wished he had use of both hands. He
enjoyed the silken smoothness of Lottie's flesh as it ran
under his fingertips. Rising up, Slocum tried to do more.
He experienced a moment of dizziness that passed.

Doubt assailed him, along with the vertigo. Slocum
wasn't sure why he was doing this. Lottie hadn't been
sleeping around with other men in Fort Griffin. Why did
she choose him? It might have been only mutual comforting, but Slocum sensed it was something more. He

had always admired Lottie Dennison. She wasn't the beauty Ellen Garland had been, but she was more mature, certain of herself—and yet there was a vulnerability he felt strongly.

And maybe he felt it in himself, too.

He gasped when her fingers curled around his stiffening manhood. She stroked up and down slowly. As he grew harder, the woman's fingers tightened and her hand worked up and down faster. He groaned as his hips began to buck.

"Not yet, not yet," she whispered hotly in his ears. "I need you. I do, John. We need each other."

Somehow, layer after layer of clothing evaporated from her. A pile of bodice and skirt and corset and petticoat appeared on the floor. Slocum ran his hand up under her camisole and found warm, trembling flesh. His fingers closed around the firm mounds of her breasts. Lottie sighed in pleasure, eyes closed and her body swaying gently. Slocum wished he could have used both hands, but his left arm was pinned under layers of bandage.

"Here, John. Stroke here," Lottie said softly. She grabbed his wrist and moved his hand lower, between her legs to the fleecy soft triangle there. His hand touched moisture, then a finger wiggled up and into her body. Lottie gasped and ground herself down into the palm of his hand. Then she stared down at him, her eyes wide.

"I want more, John. I *need* more."

She lifted her leg and threw it over his, positioning herself over his groin. She wiggled back and forth and settled down. Slocum groaned in pleasure as Lottie took his full length into her softly clutching interior.

The woman bent over and nibbled at his ear, her clever tongue darting in and out. The wet attack sent Slocum's pulse racing. He wanted to do as much for her as she was doing for him. He lifted his hips slightly and drove himself balls deep. Then he started running his hand over her back, up and down her spine, cupping her buttocks and squeezing, and racing on to find other territory to explore.

Lottie sobbed a little and started moving from his ear down to his throat and chest. Her fingers worked magic on him, tangling in his chest hair and stroking over his arms, down his flanks and all around. He lifted his hand and cupped her breast again.

The hard beating of her heart told him how aroused she was. He lost himself in the delicious sensations blasting into his body.

Lottie sensed how he was reacting. She whispered, "Hang on, John. Don't disappoint me. I need you, you need me. Together we can do anything. Together we can forget."

He lifted himself off the bed and caught her nipple between his lips. Sucking hard, Slocum cupped her left breast with his hand. He sagged back when her twisting and turning robbed him of his strength. Slocum gasped as Lottie rose up until he was just within her trembling nether lips. Then she dropped. Hard. The impact shocked him as much as it aroused him.

Slocum fought to hold back the fiery tide of his passion. He looked up and saw the hot flush rise on Lottie's breasts, up to her shoulders and to her neck. She closed her eyes and tossed her head back. Arching like a sunfishing bronco, Lottie leaned away from him so her hands rested on the bed on either side of his knees. The movement up and down now threatened to bend him in new ways. The friction burned at him and his self–control.

He started to tell her he couldn't hold back and longer when she let out a tiny gasp and shook all over. He had seen Rocky Mountain aspen leaves caught in an autumn breeze move like this. She trembled and quaked and then Slocum lost control. His hot flood blasted forth, setting off a new wave of passionate response in the woman.

She tossed her head about, her mane of long, blond hair whipping about. Then she sagged forward. Lottie put her cheek against his chest. Slocum felt hot tears running down her face and dripping onto his flesh.

"How can things be so complicated?" she asked. Slocum knew he wasn't supposed to answer, even if he could. And he couldn't. Events had a habit of running away when he wasn't paying attention. Even when he was, sometimes Slocum found himself without any means to control what happened in the world.

Ellen was dead. Willie Prentice would die for a crime he didn't commit. And now Slocum found himself in bed with Carlotta Dennison. She was a mature, handsome woman, but he wasn't sure why their lovemaking had taken place.

Comfort? Maybe. He needed it right now for his loss. But why did Lottie?

"You know where he is, don't you?" Slocum knew the lady gambler was vulnerable, but he had to finish his business with Jack Porbaugh. Only Lottie could help him.

"Jack, yes, I know. He told me." Lottie rolled off Slocum and sat on the edge of the bed, her head down. She cried openly now.

"There's no way of getting away from what we have to do," Slocum said. "We can't spend the rest of our lives like this."

Lottie turned and tried to smile. She only partly succeeded as she said, "It'd be nice to try, wouldn't it, John? You're the first man I've met in too long who's honorable." Now she did smile. "And good in bed."

"Where is Porbaugh?"

She heaved a deep breath. Slocum found himself distracted by her nakedness. Her breasts rose and fell, jiggling slightly with the movement of her shoulders. Then Lottie stood and began dressing. He saw the conflict on her face. She argued with herself about telling Slocum what he had to know.

Slocum was smart enough to know Lottie had to reach the decision on her own. Nothing he could say or do would move her if she chose not to tell him Porbaugh's whereabouts.

He pulled on his trousers and began working on his shirt and other clothing, awkward because of his broken arm. Lottie finished dressing before him and walked across the small room to stand staring out the open door.

Slocum got his boots on and was working on his gun belt when he saw the change in the woman. Carlotta Dennison took a deep breath, let it out, and turned, resolve on her face.

"Jack's just south of the Rolling Rock spread. He wants to take another five hundred head before moving on."

"Thanks," Slocum said. "I don't know if the marshal will hold up the hanging until we've caught Porbaugh, but he might be more interested in bringing a back-shooter like The Jackal to justice than hanging Prentice."

"The Jackal," mused Lottie. "That fits Jack. He's always been willing to scavenge. But don't think he's a coward, John. He's a killer. Mean and sure of himself."

"I know," Slocum said. He stopped beside her. Their eyes met and Slocum bent over slightly and kissed her. For a moment, he thought Lottie would return the kiss. Her lips lightly brushed his and then she turned away.

"You'd better go, if you want to catch him. I wish you luck. I tried to deter him by running off his men, by trying to get Willie to leave the gang. None of it worked. Jack's never going to change his ways. He'll always be the outlaw, until the day he dies."

"Lottie, thank you." Slocum started to mount his horse when she came to the door. He saw she wanted to say something more and hesitated.

"He's my husband, John."

"What?" Slocum was shocked. "Porbaugh's your husband?" Lottie only nodded before ducking back into the adobe. She closed the door with a loud slam. Slocum stood and stared for a moment, then mounted to ride back to The Flats.

Twice he had found attractive, desirable women, and both times they had been pledged to other men. Slocum wasn't sure what to make of it. Lottie Dennison.

Lottie Porbaugh.

It shook him something fierce.

"You've got to stop the hanging, marshal," Slocum pleaded. "I can find Porbaugh. He'll tell us what really happened at the stagecoach robbery. *He's* responsible, not Prentice."

"I don't doubt Porbaugh is the biggest crook unhung in Shackleford County, Slocum, but that don't change the sentence laid down by the court. Prentice swings at sundown. That's only four hours from now."

"We can get to the south side of the Rolling Rock and catch Porbaugh. He's got his gang with him. We'll need a posse—"

"I've got problems of my own," Ryder said. "Keepin' the crowd under control is gonna be a more than a handful for me. I'm a couple deputies shy right now. There's no way I'm gonna leave The Flats and go gallivantin' off across the prairie after the Porbaugh gang. My duty's clear."

"You're refusing?" Slocum hadn't considered that the marshal would flatly reject the chance to capture Porbaugh. "I *know* where he is."

"How? You one of his gang, Slocum?"

"I can't tell you how I know," Slocum said, refusing to implicate Lottie, "but I do. I tried to catch him before, but he got away." Slocum still chafed at missing his chance earlier. But even if he had spirited Jack Porbaugh away from his gang, he could never have returned to Fort Griffin in time to save Ellen.

"You and the girl was mixed up together. Everybody in town knows that, Slocum. What your interest in Prentice is, I can't rightly say. Let me tell you this, though. If you try to interfere with the execution, I'll see you danglin' next to him from those gallows. Do I make myself clear?" Ryder thrust out his chin and tried to look tough. He didn't quite succeed.

"If I bring you Porbaugh, will you at least postpone the hanging?"

"Only if you get him here with a story convincin' enough to make me fetch the judge back. That'll have to be one powerful tale."

"All right, marshal. Can't ask for anything more than that."

Ryder dismissed him with a wave of his hand. Slocum hurried outside, immediately adrift in a jeering, shouting crowd.

"Don't try to set him free, Slocum. We want to see him pay for murderin' Doc Bond," someone shouted. The Abilene Stagecoach Company manager, McGrath, forced his way to the front of the crowd and glared at Slocum.

"You heard 'em, Slocum. You might have worked as shotgun messenger for the company, but you're not showin' any loyalty now."

"Loyalty?" snorted Slocum in disgust. "You wouldn't even pay me for my work."

"I don't care what you think about me. Know that we're doin' this in memory of Doc. He was a good man. You knew him. Why are you tryin' so hard to free his killer?" McGrath didn't back down as Slocum glared at him.

"Willie Prentice is guilty of rustling," Slocum said coldly, "but he's no killer. I want Doc Bond's real murderer brought to justice. Hanging the wrong man doesn't serve justice, not if Jack Porbaugh is free to kill and rob again.''

The crowd jeered and began throwing rocks. Slocum ducked, one rock barely missing him. He tried to ignore the pain as another struck him in the left arm. A twinge of pain shot sharply through his body, then died as he swung into the saddle and looked down on the gathering. He felt a moment of anger at them, then only pity.

They did what they thought was right. Doc Bond had been a blowhard, but he was a decent man. The townspeople of Fort Griffin wanted to see his killer brought to justice. No amount of talking would ever convince them the judge hadn't sent the right man to the gallows. Only if Slocum returned with Porbaugh and a better story would they change their minds.

He tugged on the reins and got the horse trotting out of The Flats. The area south of the Rolling Rock Ranch covered quite a span, but Slocum thought he knew where Porbaugh would try to gather the cattle. Five hundred head was a considerable number, and only a few places would support that many thirsty cattle. Backtracking along the stream running across the southeastern corner of the ranch gave Slocum his best chance for finding Porbaugh and his gang.

''His gang,'' Slocum said aloud. How could he hope to fight off Porbaugh and his henchmen? He had a full cylinder in his Colt Navy, but the saddle sheath lacked a rifle, and Slocum's Winchester was still back in Abilene. Facing a dozen men or more with only six rounds and a broken arm didn't look to be all that smart. But Slocum knew he was going to try.

He was too late to save Ellen Garland. Maybe he could honor the lovely, loving, innocent girl's memory by saving her fiancé, no matter how unworthy of it Willie Prentice was.

Slocum kept scrutinizing the sun and the shadows cast in front of him as he rode. Time was running out for

Prentice. Slocum put his heels to the horse's flanks, getting a little more speed from the animal. He knew he couldn't exhaust the horse on the trip to find Porbaugh. He needed more than a moment's surge of energy to get back. Slocum had to be able to ride solid for an hour or more without the horse flagging. Still, he had to weigh the need to find Porbaugh and his gang against the return trip to town. Without the outlaw, there was no reason to go back to The Flats.

Slocum almost let out a wild cry of triumph when he saw the verge of the road. The knee–high grass had been cut up by the passage of a large number of horsemen. A cavalry patrol would have kept the destruction of the grass to a minimum, as they rode in a narrow column to maintain order. The widespread turning of the sod and crushing of the grass showed a less disciplined band of riders.

Porbaugh and his gang. It had to be. Slocum refused to believe any of Royce's cowboys had come along the road, then gone onto Rolling Rock land. They would have ridden straight out from their ranch house, coming from the north. He got more speed from his horse, then found the stream he had sought.

Strays watered as far along the stream as Slocum could see. But the main herd grazed farther to the north. He cut across country, hoping he remembered how the stream meandered. Less than a mile had passed under him before he heard loud shouts and the lowing of cattle.

Someone herded the beeves and from their loud shouts, he didn't think it was anyone riding for Royce.

Slocum topped a rise and looked down into a shallow ravine. More than a hundred head crowded into the draw. Four men carved more cattle from a bunch at the mouth and sent them running while six more kept the herd together at the bottom. The men worked well as a team, and Slocum knew they had done this many times.

He couldn't even guess how many cattle the Porbaugh gang had stolen.

He turned slowly, trying to figure out which of the riders might be Jack Porbaugh. A slow smile crossed Slocum's lips when he noticed that the leader of the gang was some distance off. He recognized Porbaugh by his shirt, remembering what the outlaw had worn before.

Slocum put heels to his horse and rode along the far side of the hill, keeping out of sight of the gang as they worked the herd. Wanting to ride hell–bent for leather, Slocum kept his eagerness under control. He would be buzzard bait if he made any mistakes. Porbaugh wanted him dead and would open fire at the first hint of trouble. And the outlaw leader wouldn't even need to know it was John Slocum approaching. All it would take was the recognition that the rider wasn't one of his own men.

Pulling up the red bandanna so it covered his face, Slocum thought this might get him a little closer before Porbaugh reacted. He rounded the hill and saw the rustler cutting out a few prime beeves from a small herd trying to drink at the stream. Porbaugh didn't see him.

Slocum rode closer, knowing he had to get within pistol range if he wanted to capture his archenemy.

Slocum thought he was going to succeed when Porbaugh turned suddenly and his pony dug in its heels. The outlaw saw Slocum. The bandanna hiding Slocum's face worked for a moment, then Porbaugh realized Slocum was not one of his own men.

Letting out a loud cry, the rustler turned his horse and rocketed off across the prairie, yelling as he went. Slocum knew he had only seconds before Porbaugh attracted the attention of his men down the draw. Taking out after the outlaw, Slocum had to stop him or die in the attempt. There wasn't a third possibility.

16

Slocum bent low and grabbed the reins in his teeth while he fumbled for the lariat tied to the right side of the saddle. He didn't want to draw and shoot. At this range and with Jack Porbaugh crouched so low in his attempt to get away, Slocum knew he could never get an accurate shot off.

More than that, Slocum didn't want Porbaugh dead. He wanted him to confess to the marshal his part in robbing the stage and killing Doc Bond. Slocum knew the outlaw might have had nothing to do with the crime, though whoever had planted the rifled strongbox among Prentice's gear to incriminate him looked mighty suspicious to Slocum. Since the only witness against Prentice rode with the Porbaugh gang, Slocum thought it was a good bet that The Jackal knew everything about the robbery and murders.

Using his knees, Slocum guided the horse as it cut

back and forth, keeping Porbaugh from getting back to his men in the draw. The thunder of cattles' hooves helped mask the commotion and drowned out the outlaw's shouts. Slocum weaved from side to side, pushing Porbaugh away from his gang.

Swinging the lariat, he tried to drop it over the rustler's head. His first toss missed. Slocum drew back the lariat, keeping his horse moving in a zigzag. He wished he had known how good this horse was at cutting. He might have sold it for a considerable sum. But the animal's training now paid off for Slocum.

Porbaugh tried to go left, but Slocum's horse cut him off. As Porbaugh turned to dodge in the other direction, Slocum awkwardly tossed the loop. It floated up and dropped gently over The Jackal's arm as if divinely guided. Slocum stood in the stirrups and caused his horse to dig in its hooves. Dirt kicked up in a choking cloud as the rope snapped taut. Porbaugh sailed through the air. He hit the ground hard, stunned for a moment by the fall.

Slocum's horse began backing, as if he had roped a calf's hind legs and worked to stretch the cow out for branding. But the rope had not settled securely. The rustler shook hard, as if he had gotten caught in a tar pot, and finally got his hand free of the lariat. He fell away heavily and crashed to his back, shouting when he landed in a patch of prickly pear cactus. This sudden release of tension on the rope caused Slocum to lose his balance.

He tumbled out of the saddle, kicking his feet hard to keep from getting his boots tangled in the stirrups. The horse bolted and charged off across the prairie, leaving Slocum stranded. He struggled to his feet and found himself facing Jack Porbaugh.

"Who the hell are you?" demanded Porbaugh. The outlaw's hand twitched and started for his six–shooter.

His eyes widened when Slocum's bandanna fell from his face. "You!"

Porbaugh drew fast. Slocum was faster. His hand blurred as it went to his Colt Navy. He had his six–gun out and sent the first shot squarely into the rustler's chest. Porbaugh gasped and struggled to finish his draw. He got his hogleg from its holster. Slocum put a second round into Porbaugh's chest.

This time, The Jackal slumped as if someone had stolen all the bones in his legs. Slocum didn't have to go to the man's side to know he had killed the only man who might clear Willie Prentice.

Slocum swung about, worried that Porbaugh's gang might have heard the gunfire. Only cattle lowed and moved around him. Slocum considered stampeding the cattle, trying to get them into the draw. So many cattle thundering into the ravine would create havoc and might save a few head from being rustled.

But Slocum knew he had other problems. He started walking and found his mount only a few yards away. A well–trained cutting horse, it stood and waited for its rider. Slocum scooped up the reins and led it back. To his surprise, Porbaugh's horse also had walked back and stood nearby. A scheme formed in his head. It wouldn't be as good as having Porbaugh confess directly to the marshal, but Slocum hoped it would slow Prentice's necktie party.

Getting Porbaugh's body heaved up and over his saddle proved almost more than Slocum could handle. Working one–handed caused more trouble than he had anticipated, but he kept at the chore and eventually hoisted Porbaugh so he could tie the rustler's body down.

Swinging into the saddle, Slocum grabbed the reins to Porbaugh's horse and started north. He dared not return directly to the road going back to Fort Griffin. The rustlers would wonder where their boss was sooner or later and come looking. Slocum bet they would be more involved with the cattle for a spell. If he rode where they could see him, with their leader's body flopped over his saddle, all hell would be out for lunch.

When he had ridden far enough, Slocum began angling across the prairie, using the gentle roll of the land to hide as much as possible. He became more aware of the way the sun dipped down. He had left The Flats four hours before Prentice's execution. Gauging the track of the sun told Slocum he had less than an hour to go. He picked up the pace and then heaved a sigh of relief when he reached the main road going into town.

Slocum rode harder, faster, pushing his horse to the limit of its endurance. Panting harshly, lather flecking its sides, the horse gave Slocum all he could hope for. He reached the edge of town with the fat red ball of the sun hanging just over the horizon.

Slocum saw the crowd gathered around the gallows and shouted, trying to attract the marshal's attention. Ryder didn't hear his cries. No one heard. The townspeople were too intent on the body swinging slowly in the afternoon breeze blowing off the prairie. The trap had been sprung and Willie Prentice had been executed.

"You poor son of a bitch," Slocum said in a low voice. He dismounted and led the horses through the crowd until he found Ryder, just coming down the steps. The marshal was pale. He might never have seen a man hanged before. Somehow, Slocum felt no sympathy for the lawman.

"I brought in Porbaugh," Slocum said. "You hung the wrong man. Prentice was innocent of killing Bond."

"Don't look much like Porbaugh's gonna tell me he done it," Ryder said, trying to appear brusque and in control of his emotions. He failed on both counts.

"His gang's rustling cattle off the Rolling Rock," Slocum said. "With a posse, you might stop them.

They're only an hour's ride outside town. Maybe a tad more.''

"That's outside my jurisdiction." Ryder tried to push past, but Slocum wouldn't let him. The marshal glowered and thrust out his chin belligerently. "What do you want from me, Slocum? I can't bring him back." Ryder jerked his thumb in the direction of Prentice's corpse. "Wouldn't if I could."

"He was guilty of rustling, nothing more," Slocum said.

"Tell it to the judge."

"What about Porbaugh? He had a bounty on his head. The judge put it there." Slocum fumed but saw nothing he could do. Shouting would gain him nothing, and it wouldn't bring back Prentice. Slocum felt a great loss, not because the boy had his neck stretched but because he had failed Ellen Garland's memory. The woman had died trying to rescue her fiancé from jail, and Slocum couldn't even save Prentice from the hangman's noose.

"I'll get you the money. Come on over to the office." Ryder walked off on shaky legs. Slocum trailed him slowly, wondering what he was going to do now. He didn't want the reward money. And he had a chore ahead of him he disliked even more than taking blood money for the rustler's death.

Slocum had found it hard to tell Ellen Garland that her betrothed had been arrested for rustling. It had been even harder sitting with a woman he had made love to as her fiancé was sentenced to hang for a crime he hadn't done. Now Slocum had to tell Carlotta Dennison her husband had been cut down in a gunfight. Fessing up to being the man who had shot Porbaugh would be even harder for Slocum.

"Leave the body out there. I don't want it smellin' up the office. As soon as I kin get Doc Woodson over here to write out a death certificate, we kin plant the son of a bitch. And you stay outside while I fetch your blood money." The marshal swatted Porbaugh's horse hard on the rump as he went by, as if this drained some of his anger at all that had happened.

Ryder vanished into his office, returning in a few minutes. His face was as bleak as an afternoon thunder storm. He shoved a sheaf of greenbacks at Slocum, as if the money burned his fingers. "Here it is. All of it. Get out of my sight."

Slocum leafed through the greenbacks, counting as he went. The marshal had overpaid him by five dollars. Slocum peeled a five off the roll and dropped it at the lawman's feet.

"You gave me too much." Slocum spun and stalked off, knowing he had to find Lottie and give her the bad news. His stride was short and he felt as if he mounted the gallows steps. Slocum walked slowly to the Lost Dutchman Dance Hall and poked his head in through the swinging doors. Tom worked at the bar, taking care of the growing crowd fresh from the hanging.

"Is Lottie upstairs yet?" Slocum asked.

Tom shook his head as he poured a round of drinks. "She's due in anytime, but I haven't seen her today. She's startin' to be flighty. Don't know what's got into her. You want to take her faro table, Slocum? I can get Curly to shuffle for you, or even hire one of those no accounts always hangin' around and—"

Slocum didn't bother listening to the rest of the saloon owner's tirade. He might not spend another night pulling numbered balls out of the goose for the keno game, either. He doubted Carlotta Dennison would be back, though Slocum wasn't sure. The lady gambler was a mysterious force in Fort Griffin. Mounting, Slocum rode through the gathering gloom to the edge of town, then headed for Lottie's house. It seemed to take an eternity to make the short ride. A few yards away from the adobe, he simply sat and stared.

Light came through one small window. He saw shadows moving inside the house and knew Lottie was still there. Had she gone to the execution or was she content to sit in her house and imagine what it was like seeing Willie Prentice's neck snapped like a chicken's?

Slocum slid from the saddle, touched the wad of greenbacks in his shirt pocket, and thought of offering Lottie the money. Slocum had no desire to keep the money for killing the woman's husband, even if Jack Porbaugh had deserved it. The few months Slocum had ridden with Porbaugh in New Mexico had convinced him the man was a cold–blooded killer. That didn't ease the obligation of telling the woman her husband was gone for all time.

Before Slocum could knock, the door opened. Lottie's face lit up in a smile when she saw him.

"John! I thought I heard someone."

"Lottie," he said, not knowing how to start. Dancing around it would do him no good. He plunged in. "I got bad news for you."

"I know about Prentice," she said in a small voice. "It's something else, isn't it? About Jack?"

"He's dead. I ran him down out on the prairie while he and his boys were rustling the Rolling Rock cattle. They were where you said they'd be." Slocum damned himself for such cowardice. He had to tell her. "I shot and killed him. Two bullets."

"He drew on you first, didn't he?" Lottie stood with no expression on her handsome face. Slocum couldn't read pain or joy. He saw nothing at all, and this bothered him as much as anything.

"He did. I don't reckon he wanted to be brought in to stand trial for his crimes."

"Don't put honey on it, John. He was an evil man."

"And he was your husband."

Lottie Dennison broke down and cried her eyes out. She ran forward and hugged Slocum tight, burying her face in his chest. He felt her hot tears soaking both shirt and the reward money in his pocket. Slocum still didn't know what to say about the bounty. And quick enough he found himself being pulled inside.

"I need comforting, John. I know you can do it. I helped you when Ellen was killed. Help me now." Lottie began unbuttoning her blouse.

Slocum stared at her for a moment, reflecting that he had turned her into a widow. He owed her something. Slocum helped her forget.

17

Slocum's dreams bothered him. He fought and thrashed about, his hand reaching for his six–shooter. Sitting up in the small bed, Slocum found he was alone in the adobe house. He shook away the sleep lingering with the disturbing images of him shooting Jack Porbaugh and pulling the handle that sent Willie Prentice to his maker and gunning down Ellen Garland. Slocum struggled to force away the last of the confusing mix of nightmarish images.

He swung his long legs over the edge of the bed and stretched. His arm didn't hurt nearly as much as it had the day before when he had fought Porbaugh. Slocum knew he was healing slowly. Looking around the room, he tried to figure where Lottie had gotten to.

"Lottie!" he called, worried that she might have done something stupid. She had been shaken hearing her husband was dead. Slocum wasn't sure if he had done the right thing sleeping with her, but it seemed to have calmed them both down.

"Getting some water, John," Lottie said, coming into the room with two buckets sloshing over onto the floor. She dumped the contents into a large wooden tub. "Need it for cooking and the like."

"Lottie?" He finished pulling on his trousers. He went to her, not sure what to say. "Let me do this. You've had quite a jolt hearing your husband is dead and all." Slocum knew it sounded lame, but the words didn't form right. He thought highly of her and didn't want to hurt her any more.

"I'm no hothouse flower, John," she said. A slight smile danced at her lips and then disappeared. "He was my husband. I married Jack when I was only seventeen."

Slocum blinked. He didn't know how old she was, but he reckoned Lottie had to be almost thirty. When he had ridden with Porbaugh in New Mexico The Jackal hadn't said anything about being married.

"A long time, I know. I was young and he was so dashing. He was in the war, you know. A colonel he said."

"Porbaugh? No, I don't think so," Slocum said. Slocum had ridden with Quantrill's Raiders and had risen to the rank of captain with the partisans. Nothing about Porbaugh told of military discipline, even the loose kind exercised by Quantrill and Bloody Bill Anderson and Little Archie Clement.

"I don't think he was, either. The more I came to know Jack, the more I realized not much of what he said was true. I thought he was a rancher." She let out a bitter laugh. "He always smelled of cattle and he told me about this fabulous spread of his. He was a rustler and nothing more. A thief and a liar." Bitterness tinged her words now.

"But you loved him, didn't you?"

Lottie shrugged. "Can't rightly say. Once I did, but he always provoked me so. That's why I tried to steer Willie away from his gang. And I tried to get the others to leave him, too, but they were all hard men, outlaws through and through. Maybe I thought Jack would go straight if he lost his men. Foolishness, I know, but that's the way it might have been in my head."

She studied Slocum's furrowed brow and reached out to brush her fingers along his cheek. "Don't fret so, John. I don't blame you for killing him. If you said it was a fair fight, I believe it. If it had been the other way around, I'd've known Jack was lying."

"It's important to me that you don't hold me responsible."

"I don't," she said, sighing heavily. "I came out here looking for him to get a divorce, but I still loved him in a way. You never forget your first love, and Jack Porbaugh was that for me. Oh, how he could sweet–talk me!"

Slocum kept silent as he struggled into the rest of his clothes. Lottie spun tales of how she and Porbaugh had ridden together for a while. She had learned to deal faro and poker with him, then he had upped and left her. Everything the man had done hurt her a little more.

"What of Prentice and Ellen Garland?" Slocum asked. "How'd you know them?"

"I met Willie through Jack. He talked constantly of Ellen and I tried to argue him out of riding with Jack. Jack thought that was funny. He had the boy wrapped around his little finger, what with tales of living high down in Mexico and never getting caught by the law no matter how much they rustled."

"What are you going to do now?"

"Why, I'll see to his burial. He was my husband." Lottie brushed off her hands and said, "You're decent. Let's go into town so I can make the arrangements. One of Dr. Woodson's in–laws is the undertaker. I am sure he will see to Jack's body with all possible decency.''

"It's more than he deserves, the way he treated you," Slocum said. Now he felt no regret for having cut down Jack Porbaugh. Hearing how the outlaw had treated his wife made Slocum even happier he had ended the rustler's sordid life.

"Go out and get my buggy hitched up, will you? I have a few things to tend to before we go."

Slocum went outside and found a small stable with a sturdy horse inside nibbling away at a bale of hay. He led the horse out and hitched it to a buggy. In the rear of the buggy a tarpaulin covered a large pile. He started to pull it back to see what lay under it when Lottie came out.

"Ready, John?"

"Purt near," he said, cinching up the leather for her. He helped the woman into the buggy, then mounted his own horse. Side by side they rode into Fort Griffin. Slocum's mind turned over dozens of things he wanted to do and say. Somehow, they all got confused.

He had been taken with Ellen, but the shock of finding she had been pledged to another had hit him like being dealt five aces. He was pleased as punch about being in the game, yet he knew anyone seeing his hand would know he was cheating. And it didn't stop there. He had lain with another man's wife.

Then he had killed Jack Porbaugh, making Lottie a widow.

Slocum had feelings for Carlotta Dennison but had a devil of a time sorting out what they might be. They helped each other out in their need, but did it go farther than that? Slocum was at a loss to say.

"There's the digger man," Lottie said, pointing to the mortician's office down an alley. "I'll see to it."

Slocum waited as the Abilene Stagecoach Company's daily Concord rattled into town. It would be on its way south to San Antonio in less than ten minutes. The stage would take on mail, passengers, and luggage and be off on its dusty trip across the belly of Texas. Slocum rubbed his arm, knowing he could still be getting twenty dollars a ride as shotgun messenger if things had worked out differently. Slocum shrugged it off. He had a decent enough job at the Lost Dutchman while he healed.

And there was Lottie Dennison. More and more he was coming around to thinking of her as part of his future.

"John. John!"

"What?" He turned to her. He had been daydreaming.

"Take this letter. Open it after you pick up my pay from Tom. The money should be put to good use."

Slocum glanced into the undertaker's office and nodded absently, his thoughts still wandering. He knew what she needed the money for. Slocum hitched his horse on the street, walked around the stagecoach unloading its passengers, and headed for the saloon.

Tom stood behind the long bar, polishing its wooden surface bar with a greasy rag. He frowned when he saw Slocum.

"Wondered if you would ever show up. You left me in the lurch. Where were you last night?"

"With Lottie," Slocum said, not wanting to say any more. "She sent me over for her pay. From the way you're acting, maybe I'd better get mine, too."

"Yeah," Tom said, fishing under the bar. He pulled out a cigar box and opened it. He scowled as he counted out two piles of money. "That's yours, this is for Lottie. Reckon it's okay to give it to you."

"I got her authorization here," Slocum said, tapping the letter. Tom pushed it back.

"I trust you, even if you didn't show up. We lost a heap of money last night. It was real good after the hangin'."

Slocum pushed a dime back and asked for a drink.

Outside, the driver bellowed for passengers to board the stage. Tom shoved across the drink and gave back Slocum's dime.

"Hell, Slocum, I don't want you quittin' on me. You're good."

"And you think if I talk to Lottie she'll stay?"

"Something like that," Tom said dolefully. "Losin' her will hurt something fierce."

Slocum knocked back the whiskey and let it burn all the way down to his belly. The aches and pains he felt dissolved, and he found himself thinking more clearly.

"I'll see what I can do, Tom," he said. Slocum considered a second drink, then decided against it. Scooping up the money from the bar, Slocum left the Lost Dutchman. Outside on the boardwalk he coughed, choking on the dust from the departing stagecoach. He walked slowly back to the mortician's, not wanting anything to do with planning services for the likes of Jack Porbaugh. But for Lottie's sake, he would stand by her.

After fifteen minutes, Slocum got antsy. He entered the small office, but Lottie was nowhere to be seen.

The undertaker looked up, hound dog sad eyes turned to Slocum. The man smiled, but there was no amity to it.

"How may I serve you, sir?"

"I'm looking for Miss Dennison," Slocum said. Seeing no recognition on the undertaker's face, Slocum changed it. "Mrs. Porbaugh. She came in a while back to arrange for her husband's funeral."

"Ah, yes, Mrs. Porbaugh."

"I have the money for the funeral." Slocum dug in his pocket to get Lottie's wages. He reckoned he could add the hundred he had made from killing Porbaugh. She need never know.

"Why, sir, it is all paid for. In cash."

"Where is she?" Slocum thought there might be a private room for viewing the body.

"She left in quite a hurry."

Slocum dashed out of the mortician's office and saw Lottie's buggy still parked at the mouth of the alley. He went to it and immediately noticed the tarp lay flat. Whatever had been underneath was gone. Suddenly suspicious, Slocum ran to the stage depot. McGrath sat behind the ticket window, slowly counting money from a tin box. He frowned when Slocum came up.

"Lottie. Lottie Dennison," demanded Slocum. "Have you seen her?"

"The gamblin' lady from the saloon? She got on the stage. Bound for San Antone, I reckon."

Slocum ran outside, thinking to jump onto his horse and chase after the stage. He paused for a moment, his hand touching the envelope in his pocket. Slocum remembered what she had actually said to him. Lottie had told him to open it after he'd collected her wages from Tom, not use the letter as authorization for Tom to pay the wages. Slocum pulled out the rumpled letter and awkwardly tore it open.

His eyes scanned down the page quickly. It read:

Dear John,
    How can I ever thank you for all your kindness? Leaving like a thief in the night is no way to repay you, but I can think of no words. It is easier for me this way.
    Please do not think poorly of me.
    Take my pay and all my belongings and give them to charity. And again, thank you for being so accepting.

                                    Carlotta

Slocum reread the letter, then shoved it into his pocket. He mounted and rode back to her house, thinking she might somehow have returned there. The first thing he noticed when he burst into the small adobe was her missing chest. A quick search showed all her clothing gone. He sat on the narrow bed where they had made love and stared at a blank wall for some time.

Then he left, riding to the church where Lottie had never missed a Sunday service. It took a few minutes for him to convince the pastor that Lottie wanted those less fortunate to have the benefit of her possessions.

"She was a generous lady," Reverend Trenchard said.

"This is part of it, too," Slocum said, counting out Lottie's pay. His fingers touched his shirt pocket. He pulled out the greenbacks he had gotten for gunning down Jack Porbaugh. "This, also. She'd like you to have it all." Slocum recollected how Marshal Ryder had called the bounty blood money. And it was. It felt unclean as long as it was in his hands. Letting the pastor put it to good use seemed the only way to make Jack Porbaugh repay some of the debts he had amassed.

Slocum listened to the pastor's profuse gratitude for a few minutes, then excused himself. He climbed into the saddle and rode to the main road. South and west went to Abilene. There his rifle still rested in a hotel room. But to the south traveled Lottie Dennison.

"That's one fine rifle. I'd hate to lose it," he said to his horse. The animal crow-hopped a mite. Slocum kept it under control and turned its face south, toward San Antonio.

And Lottie Dennison. Slocum wasn't sure what he'd say to her when he caught up, but he did know she was the only good thing to happen to him in Fort Griffin. Putting his heels to his horse's flanks, Slocum started the long ride after her.